PENGUIN BOOKS

We Live in Water

'Walter is a bighearted man who excels at writing about other bighearted, if broken, men. That generosity of spirit coupled with Walter's seeming inability to look away from the messy bits, elevates these stories from dirges to symphonies' *New York Times Book Review*

'Stories that twist and plumb, delivering unexpected laughs while playing with what it is we think we know . . . Walter has emerged as one of the country's most dazzling novelists' *Seattle Times*

'Wildly entertaining and thought-provoking fiction from a prodigiously talented writer' *Booklist*

'Gritty, big-hearted' *Esquire*

'Walter's got a great ear and a genius for sympathy with America's new dispossessed' *NPR*

'Brims with humanity' *Entertainment Weekly*

'Gritty, pitch perfect . . . wrings enlightenment from dark realities' *People*

'A prodigiously gifted writer' *Los Angeles Review of Books*

ABOUT THE AUTHOR

Jess Walter is the author of six novels, including *The Financial Lives of the Poets*, published by Penguin. *Beautiful Ruins* was a number one *New York Times* bestseller. *We Live in Water* is his first collection of short fiction. Jess Walter lives in Spokane, Washington with his family.

We Live in Water

Stories

JESS WALTER

PENGUIN BOOKS

PENGUIN BOOKS

Published by the Penguin Group
Penguin Books Ltd, 80 Strand, London WC2R 0RL, England
Penguin Group (USA) Inc., 375 Hudson Street, New York, New York 10014, USA
Penguin Group (Canada), 90 Eglinton Avenue East, Suite 700, Toronto, Ontario, Canada M4P 2Y3
(a division of Pearson Penguin Canada Inc.)
Penguin Ireland, 25 St Stephen's Green, Dublin 2, Ireland
(a division of Penguin Books Ltd)
Penguin Group (Australia), 707 Collins Street, Melbourne, Victoria 3008, Australia
(a division of Pearson Australia Group Pty Ltd)
Penguin Books India Pvt Ltd, 11 Community Centre,
Panchsheel Park, New Delhi – 110 017, India
Penguin Group (NZ), 67 Apollo Drive, Rosedale, Auckland 0632, New Zealand
(a division of Pearson New Zealand Ltd)
Penguin Books (South Africa) (Pty) Ltd, Block D, Rosebank Office Park,
181 Jan Smuts Avenue, Parktown North, Gauteng 2193, South Africa

Penguin Books Ltd, Registered Offices: 80 Strand, London WC2R 0RL, England

www.penguin.com

First published in the United States of America by Harper Perennial 2013
First published in Penguin Books 2014
001

Copyright © Jess Walter, 2013
All rights reserved

The moral right of the author has been asserted

'Anything Helps' appeared in *McSweeney's* and in *The Best American Short Stories 2012*. 'We Live in Water'
appeared in *Playboy*. 'Thief' appeared in *Harper's*. 'Can a Corn' appeared in *The Flash* and *Forty Stories*.
'Virgo' appeared in *Portland Noir*. 'Helpless Little Things' appeared in *Playboy*. 'Please' appeared in *Willow
Springs*. 'Don't Eat Cat' appeared in *Byliner* and in *The Best American Nonrequired Reading 2012*. 'The New
Frontier' appeared in *Fugue*. 'The Wolf and the Wild' appeared in *McSweeney's*. 'Wheelbarrow Kings'
appeared in *The Speed Chronicles*. 'Statistical Abstract for My Hometown of Spokane, Washington'
appeared in *McSweeney's*.

Printed in Great Britain by Clays Ltd, St Ives plc

Except in the United States of America, this book is sold subject
to the condition that it shall not, by way of trade or otherwise, be lent,
re-sold, hired out, or otherwise circulated without the publisher's
prior consent in any form of binding or cover other than that in
which it is published and without a similar condition including this
condition being imposed on the subsequent purchaser

ISBN: 978-0-241-00385-5

www.greenpenguin.co.uk

MIX
Paper from
responsible sources
FSC
www.fsc.org   FSC™ C018179

Penguin Books is committed to a sustainable
future for our business, our readers and our planet.
This book is made from Forest Stewardship
Council™ certified paper.

To Warren and Cal

CONTENTS

ANYTHING HELPS

BIT HATES going to cardboard.

But he got tossed from the Jesus beds for drunk and sacrilege, and he's got no other way to get money. So he's up behind Frankie Doodle's, flipping through broken-down produce boxes like an art buyer over a rack of paintings, and when he finds a piece without stains or writing he rips it down until it's square. Then he walks to the Quik Stop, where the fat checker likes him. He flirts her out of a Magic Marker and a beefstick.

The beefstick he eats right away and cramps his gut. He sets the cardboard on the counter and writes carefully in block letters: ANYTHING HELPS. The checker says, You got good handwriting, Bit.

The best spot, where the freeway lets off next to Dicks, is taken by some chalker Bit's never seen before: skinny, dirty pants, hollow eyes. The kid's sign reads HOMELESS HUNGRY. Bit yells, *Homeless Hungry?* Dude, I *invented* Homeless Hungry. The kid just waves.

Bit walks on, west toward his other spot. There are a few others out, stupid crankers—faces stupid, signs stupid: some forty-year-old baker with VIETNAM VET, too dumb to know he wasn't born yet, and a coke ghost with tiny writing—*Can You Help me feed My Children please.* They're at stupid intersections, too, with synced lights so the cars never stop.

Bit's headed to his unsynced corner—fewer cars, but at least they have to stop. Streamers off the freeway, working people, South Hill kids, ladies on their way to lunch. When he gets there he grabs the light pole and sits back against it, eyes down—nonthreatening, pathetic. It feels weird; more than a year since he's had to do this. You think you're through with some things.

He hears a window hum and gets up, walks to the car without making eye contact. Gets a buck. Thank you. Minute later, another car, another window, another buck. Bless you.

Good luck, the people always say.

For the next hour, it's a tough go. Cars come off the hill, hit the light, stop, look, leave. A woman who looks at first like Julie glances over and mouths, I'm sorry. Bit mouths back: Me too. Most people stare straight ahead, avoid eye contact.

After a while a black car stops, and Bit stands. But when the windows come down it's just some boys in ball caps. Worst kind of people are boys in ball caps. Bit should just be quiet, but—

You stinking fucking drunk.

Yeah, I get that sometimes.

Why don't you get a job?

Good advice. Thanks.

A couple of nickels fly out the window and skitter against the curb; the boys yell some more. Bit waits until they drive away to get the nickels, carefully. He's heard of kids heating coins with their cigarette lighters. But the nickels are cool to the touch. Bit sits against his pole. A slick creeps down his back.

Then a guy in a gold convertible Mercedes almost makes the light but has to slam on his brakes.

I think you could've made it, Bit says.

The guy looks him over. Says, You look healthy enough to work.

Thanks. So do you.

Let me guess—veteran?

Yep. War of 1812.

The guy laughs. Then what, you lost your house?

Misplaced it.

You're a funny fucker. Hey, tell you what. I'll give you twenty bucks if you tell me what you're gonna buy with it.

The light changes but the guy just sits there. A car goes around. Bit shields his eyes from the sun.

You give me twenty bucks?

Yeah, but you can't bullshit me. If I give you a twenty, honestly, what are you gonna get?

The new Harry Potter book.

You are one funny fucker.

Thanks. You too.

No. Tell me *exactly* what you're going to drink or smoke or whatever, and I'll give you twenty. But it's gotta be the truth.

The truth. Why does everyone always want that? He looks at the guy in his gold convertible. Back at the Jesus Beds they'll be gathering for group about now, trying to talk one another out of this very thing, this reverie, truth.

Vodka, Bit says, because it fucks you up fastest. I'll get it at the store over on Second, whatever cheap stuff they got, plastic in case I drop it. And I'll get a bag of nuts or pretzels.

Something solid to shit later. Whatever money's left—Bit's mouth is dry—I'll put in municipal bonds.

After the guy drives off, Bit looks down at the twenty-dollar bill in his hand. Maybe he is a Funny Fucker.

BIT SLIDES the book forward. *Harry Potter and the Deathly Hallows*. What's a hallow, anyway? he asks.

The clerk takes the book and runs it through the scanner. I guess it's British for hollow. I don't read those books.

I read the first one. It was pretty good. Bit looks around Auntie's Bookstore: big and open, a few soft chairs between the rows of books. So what do *you* read?

Palahniuk. That'll be twenty-eight fifty-six.

Bit whistles. Counts out the money and sets it on the counter. Shit, he thinks, seventy cents short.

The clerk has those big loopy earrings that stretch out your lobes. He moves his mouth as he counts the money.

How big are you gonna make those holes in your ears?

Maybe like quarter-size. Hey, you're a little short. You got a discount card?

Bit pats himself down. Hmm. In my other pants.

Be right back, the kid says, and leaves with the book.

I'm kind of in a hurry, Bit says to the kid's back.

He needs to stop by the Jesus Beds, although he knows Cater might not let him in. He likes Cater, in spite of the guy's mean-Jesus rules and intense, mean-Jesus eyes. It's a shame what happened, because Bit had been doing so good, going to group almost every day, working dinner shifts and in the yard. Cater has this pay system at the Jesus Beds, where you serve or clean or do yard work and get paid in these vouchers that you redeem for snacks and shit at the little store they run. Keeps everything kind of in-house and gets people used to spending their money on something other than getting fucked up. Of course, there's a side market in the vouchers, dime on the dollar, so over time people save enough to get stewed, but Bit's been keeping that under control, too, almost like a civilian. No crank for more than a year, just a beer or two once a month, occasionally a split bottle of wine.

Then last weekend happened. At group on Thursday, Fat Danny had been bragging again about the time he OD'd, and that made Bit think of Julie, the way her foot kept twitching after she stopped breathing, so after group he took a couple of bucks from his stash—the hollow rail of his bed—and had a beer. In a tavern. Like a real person, leaned up against the bar watching baseball. And it was great. Hell, he didn't even drink all of it; it was more about the bar than the beer.

But it tasted so good he broke down on Friday and got two forties at the Quik Stop. And when he came back to the Jesus Beds, Wallace ran off to Cater and told him Bit sold his vouchers for booze money.

Consequences, Cater is always saying.

I feel shitty, Bit's always saying.

Let's talk about *you*, Andrea the social worker is always saying.

When you sober up come see me, the fat checker at the Quik Stop is always saying.

Funny fucker, the guy in the gold convertible is always saying.

The bookstore kid finally comes back. He's got a little card, like a driver's license, and he gives it to Bit with a pen. There, now you have a discount card, the kid says. On the little piece of cardboard, where it says NAME, Bit writes, *Funny Fucker*. Where it says ADDRESS, Bit writes: *Anything Helps*.

BIT STARTS walking again, downtown along the river. For a while, he and Julie camped farther down the bank, where the water turns and flattens out. They'd smoke and she'd lie back and mumble about getting their shit together.

Bit tried to tell Cater that. Yes, he'd fucked up, but he'd actually been selling his vouchers to buy this book, to get his shit together. But Cater was suspicious, asked a bunch of questions, and then Wallace piped in with *He's lying* and Bit lunged at Wallace and Cater pulled him off—rough about it, too—Bit yelling *Goddamn this* and *Goddamn that*, making it three-for-three (1. No drinking, 2. No fighting, 3. No taking the Lord's etc.), so that Cater had no choice, he said, rules being rules.

Then I got no choice either, Bit said, pacing outside the Jesus Beds, pissed off.

Sure you do, Cater said. You always have a choice.

Of course, Cater was right. But out of spite or self-pity, or just thirst, Bit went and blew half his book money on a fifth, spent a couple of nights on the street and then shot the rest of his money on another. You think you're through with some things, picking smokes off the street, shitting in alleys. He woke this morning in a parking lot above the river, behind a humming heat pump. Looked down at the river and could practically see Julie lying back in the grass. *When we gonna get our shit together, Wayne?*

Bit walks past brick apartments and empty warehouses. Spokane's a donut city, downtown a hole, civilians all in the suburbs. *Donut City* is part of Bit's *unifying urban theory*, like the part about how every failing downtown tries the same stupid fixes: hang a vertical sign on an empty warehouse announcing *Luxury Lofts!*, buy buses that look like trolley cars, open a shitty farmers' market.

Very interesting, Andrea says whenever Bit talks about his theory. But we talk about *ourselves* at group, Bit. Let's talk about you.

But what if this *is* me? Bit asked once. Why can't we be the things that we see and think? Why do we always have to be these sad stories, like Fat Danny pretending he's sorry he screwed up his life when we all know he's really just bragging about how much coke he used to do? Why can't we talk about *what we think* instead of just all the stupid shit we've *done*?

Okay, Wayne, she said—what do you think?

I think I've done some real stupid shit.

Andrea likes him, always laughs at his jokes, treats him smarter than the group, which he is. She even flirts with him, a little.

Where's your nickname come from? she asked him one time.

It's because that's all a woman can take of my wand, he said. Just a bit. Plus I chewed a man to death once. Bit right through his larynx.

It's his last name is all, said Wallace. Bittinger.

That's true, he said. Although I did bite a guy's larynx once.

You think you're so smart, Wallace is always saying.

And do you want to talk about Julie? Andrea is always saying.

Not so much, Bit's always saying.

We're all children before God, Cater is always saying.

But Cater isn't even at the Jesus Beds when Bit stops there. He's at his kid's soccer game. Kenny the Intake Guy leans out the window and says he can't let Bit in the door till he clears it with Cater.

Sure, Bit says, just do me a favor. He takes the book from the bag. Tell him I showed you this.

BIT WALKS past brick storefronts and apartments, through nicer neighborhoods with green lawns. The book's heavy under his arm.

Another part of Bit's unifying urban theory is sprinklers, that you can gauge a neighborhood's wealth by the way people water. If every single house has an automatic system, you're looking at a six-figure mean. If the majority lug hoses around, it's more lower-middle class. And if they don't bother with the lawns . . . well, that's the sort of shitburg where Bit and Julie always lived, except for that little place they rented in Wenatchee the summer Bit worked at the orchard. He sometimes thinks back to that place and imagines what it would be like if he could undo everything that came after that point, like standing up a line of dominos. All the way back to Nate.

Bit breathes deeply, looks around at the houses to get his mind off it, at the sidewalks and the garden bricks and the homemade mailboxes. It isn't a bad walk. The Molsons live in a neighborhood between arterials, maybe ten square blocks of '50s and '60s ranchers and ramblers, decent-sized edged yards, clean, the sort of block Julie always liked—nice but not overreaching. Bit pulls out the postcard, reads the address again even though he remembers the place from last time. Two more blocks.

It's getting cool, heavy clouds settling down like a blanket over a kid. It'll rain later. Bit puts this neighborhood at about 40 percent sprinkler systems, 25 percent two-car garages, lots of rock gardens and lined sidewalks. The Molsons have the biggest house on the block, gray, two-story with a big addition on back. Two little boys—one black, one white, both littler than Nate—are in the front yard, behind a big cyclone fence, bent over something. A bug, if Bit had to bet.

Hullo, Bit says from his side of the fence. You young gentlemen know if Nate's around?

He's downstairs playing Ping-Pong, says one of the boys. The other grabs his arm, no doubt heeding a warning about stranger-talk.

Maybe you could tell Mr. or Mrs. Molson that Wayne Bittinger's outside. Here to see Nate for one half-a-second is all.

The boys are gone a while. Bit clears his throat. Shifts his weight. Listens for police. He looks around the neighborhood and it makes him sad that it's not nicer, that Nate didn't get some South Hill fosters, a doctor or something. Stupid thought; he's embarrassed for having it.

Mrs. Molson looks heavier than the last time he stopped, in the spring—has it been that long? More than half a year? She's shaped like a bowling pin, with a tuft of side-swooped hair and big round glasses. A saint, though, she and her husband both, for taking in all these kids.

She frowns. Mr. Bittinger—

Please, call me Wayne.

Mr. Bittinger, I told you before, you can't just stop by here.

No, I know that, Mrs. Molson. I'm supposed to go through the guardian ad litem. I know. I just . . . his birthday got away from me. I wanted to give him a book. Then I swear, I'll—

What book? She holds out her hands. Bit hands it over. She opens the bag, looks in without taking the book out, like it might be infected.

Mr. Bittinger, you *know* how Mr. Molson and I feel about these books. She tries to hand it back to him, but Bit won't take it.

No, I know, Mrs. Molson. He pats the postcard in his back pocket—picture of a lake and a campground. It was mailed to their old apartment. Bit's old landlord Gayle brought it down to the Jesus Beds for him, what, a month ago—or was it three months now?

Dad — I'm at camp and we're supposed to write our parents and I'm kind of mad (not really just a little) at the Molsons for taking away my Harry Potter books which they think are Satanic. I did archery here which was fun. I hope you're doing good too. Nate.

I respect your beliefs, Bit tells Mrs. Molson. I do. It's probably why you and Mr. Molson are such good people, to open your home up like this. But Nate, he loves them Harry Potter books. And after all he's been through, me being such a fuckup—Jesus, why did he say that—I'm sorry, pardon my . . . and losing his mother, I just . . . I mean . . . Bit can feel his face flushing.

Mrs. Molson glances back at the house. For what it's worth, we don't push our beliefs on the boys, Mr. Bittinger, she says. It's all about rules. Everyone here goes to church and everyone spends an hour on homework and we monitor closely what they read and watch. We have the same rules for all the boys. Otherwise it doesn't work. Not with eight of them.

No, I could see that, Bit says. I could.

Bit read the first Harry Potter to Nate when he was only six, even doing a British accent sometimes. Julie read him the second one, no accent, but cuddled up in the hotel bed where they were crashing. They got the books from the library. After the second one, Nate started reading them himself. Bit kind of wishes he'd kept up with the books, before the dominos started going: before CPS came, before Julie got so hopeless and strung out, before . . .

We've been doing this a long time, Mrs. Molson is saying. We've had upwards of forty foster kids, and we've found that this is what works: adherence to rules.

Yep, that's how we saw things, too, and I can't tell you how much I appreciate him having a stable home like this. I really do. My wife and I, we did our best, and we always figured that once we got everything back together, that, uh . . . but of course . . .

Mrs. Molson looks down at her shoes.

This wasn't what he meant to do, this self-pity. He wanted to talk like real people, but Bit feels himself fading. It's like trying to speak another language—conversational Suburban—and it tires him out the way group does: everybody crying their bullshit about the choices they've made and the clarity they've found. And he's worse than any of them, wanting so bad for Andrea to like him, to think he's fixed, when all he really wants is a pinch, or a pint.

Bit clears his throat.

It's just . . . you know, this one thing. I don't know.

Mr. Bittinger—

Finally, Bit smiles, and rasps: Anything helps.

She looks up at him with what must be pity, although he can't quite make it out. Then she sighs and looks down at the book again. I guess . . . I could put it away for him. For later. He can have it when you can take him again . . . or when he's on his own, or someone else—

Thank you. I'd appreciate that. Bit clears his throat. But before you put it away, could you show it to him? Tell him his old man brought it for his birthday?

Sure, Mrs. Molson says, and then she gets hard again. But Mr. Bittinger, you can't come by here.

I know that, he says.

Next time I'll call the police.

He begins backing away. Won't be a next time.

You said that last spring.

Backing away: I know. I'm sorry.

Call Mr. Gandor, and I'm sure he'll set up a visitation.

I will. Thank you, Mrs. Molson.

She turns and goes inside. Bit stands where he's backed, middle of the street, feels like he's about to burst open, a water balloon or a sack of fluid, gush out onto the pavement and trickle down to the curb. *When are we gonna get our shit together?*

Quickly, Bit begins walking toward downtown. He imagines the curtains parting in the houses around him. *Think you're so smart. Let's talk about you.* Jesus he wants something. He stowed his ANYTHING HELPS sign back behind Frankie Doodle's; instead of going to the Jesus Beds and pleading with Cater, maybe he'll go get his sign. Hit that corner again. Tear it up one more night, like him and Julie used to. Maybe the guy in the gold convertible will come back and give him another twenty. He tries to think of something good. Imagines the guy in the gold Mercedes pulling up and Bit spinning his sign and it reading *Funny Fucker* and the guy laughing and Bit jumping in the car and them going to get totally fucked up in Reno or someplace.

Anything helps funny fucker! Funny fucker helps anything! You want to talk about Julie? Fuck funny anything helps! How long you been saving for that book, Bit? Anything funny helps fucker!

Dad! Bit turns and there's Nate, stand-pedaling a little BMX bike up the street, its frame swinging beneath his size. Jeez, he's big, and he's got a bike? Of course he does. What thirteen-year-old doesn't have a bike? He remembers Julie waking up once, saying, We gotta get Nate a bike. Even fucked up, Bit knew that not having a bike was the least of the kid's problems.

He tries to focus. The kid's hair is so short, like a military cut. Julie would hate that. There's something else—his teeth. He's got braces on. When he pulls up Bit sees he's got the book in its brown bag under his arm.

I can't take this, Dad.

No, it's okay, Bit says. I talked to Mrs. Molson and she said—

I read it at camp. This kid in my cabin had it. It was good. But you should take it back.

Bit closes his eyes against a wave of dizziness. No, Nate, I want you to have it.

Really, he says, I can't. I'm sorry. And he holds it out, making direct eye contact, like a cop. Jesus, Bit thinks, the kid's different in every way—taller and so . . . awake.

Take it, Nate says. Please.

Bit takes it.

I shouldn't have wrote that in my postcard, Nate says. I was mad they wouldn't let me read the book, but I understand it now. I was being stupid.

No, Bit says, I was glad you sent that card. You have a good birthday?

It seems to take a minute for Nate to recall his birthday. Oh. Yeah. It was cool. We went to the water slides.

And school starts . . .

Three weeks ago.

Oh. Sure, he says, but he can't believe it. It's not like time passes anymore; it leaks, it seeps. Bit wants to say something about the grade, just so Nate knows *he knows*. He counts years in his head: one after they took Nate, one after Julie, and one he's been trying to get better in the Jesus Beds—a little more than three years the Molsons have had him. Jesus.

So . . . you nervous about eighth grade?

Nah. I was more nervous last year.

Yeah. Bit can barely take this steady eye contact. It reminds him of Cater.

Consequences, Cater's always saying.

I was more nervous last year, Nate's always saying.

I don't feel good, Julie's always saying.

Yeah, Bit says, no need to be nervous. He's still in danger of bursting, bleeding over the street.

You okay, Dad?

Sure. Just glad I got to see you. That ad litem business . . . I'm not good at planning ahead.

It's okay. Nate smiles. Looks back over his shoulder. Well . . . I should—

Yeah. Bit moves to hug the boy or shake his hand or something, but it's like the kid's a mile away. Hey, good luck with school, and everything.

Thanks. Then Nate pedals away. He looks back once, and is gone.

Bit breathes. He stands on the street. Imagines the curtains on the street fluttering. What if Julie didn't die? What if she got herself one of these houses and she's watching him now? *You ever gonna get your shit together, Bit? You gonna get Nate back? Or you goin' back to cardboard?*

Bit looks down at the book in his hands.

At the Jesus Beds last weekend, after Bit explained to Cater how he was only a couple dollars short of buying this book for his kid, Cater stared at him in the most pathetic way.

What? Bit asked.

Cater said, How long you been saving for that book, Bit?

What do you mean?

I mean, ask yourself, how long you been a couple dollars short?

He supposes that's why he went crazy, Cater always looking at him like he's kidding himself. Like he's always thinking, How long has it been since you saw your kid, anyway?

BIT STANDS outside the bookstore holding a twenty-eight-dollar book. Holding twenty-eight dollars. Holding three fifths of vodka. Holding nine forty-ounce beers. Holding five bottles of fortified wine. Holding his boy. Civilians go into the store and come out carrying books in little brown bags just like the one he's got in his hands.

Here's why at the Jesus Beds they can only talk about all the stupid shit they've done—because that's all they are now, all they're ever gonna be, a twitching bunch of memories and mistakes, regrets. Jesus, he thinks. I should've had the decency to go when Julie did.

BIT EASES against the light pole. You think you're through with some things. But you aren't.

It's about to rain; the cars coming off the freeway have their windows up. It's fine, though. Bit likes the cool wet air.

The very first car pauses at the bottom of the hill and its driver, a woman, glances over. Bit looks away, opens the thick book and begins reading.

The two men appeared out of nowhere, a few yards apart
in the narrow, moonlit lane. For a second they stood quite
still, wands pointing at each other's chests . . .

The light changes but the woman doesn't go. Raindrops have started to dapple the page, so Bit pulls his jacket over his head, to shield the book. And when he goes back to reading, this time it's with the accent and everything.

WE LIVE IN WATER

1958

OREN DESSENS leaned forward as he drove, perched on the wheel, cigarette in the corner of his mouth, open can of beer between his knees. He'd come apart before, of course, a couple three times, maybe more, depending on how you counted. The way Katie figured—every fistfight and whore, every poker game and long drunk—he was always coming apart, but Oren didn't think it was fair to count like his ex-wife did. Up to him, he'd only count those times he was in real danger of not coming back. Like that morning on the carrier.

"Dad?"

He'd technically been at war the whole four months he was out, but he'd only been in danger that one time, a month before the end, a beautiful dawn in open water, up deck with his slop crew, alone as a man could feel, the planes huddled at one end of the gray deck like birds, wings-up. The rest of the world, in every direction, seemed like bands of varying blue, except for a thin gray line where the sea and sky met, and then the horn sounded and a single, smoking plane fell out of nowhere—no Japanese carrier or base anywhere nearby—just a lost Zeke falling out of that deep blue like a single raindrop, twisting for the deck, coming so close Oren could see the red suns on the wings before the thing dropped harmlessly off the stern—an osprey going for a fish.

"Dad?"

But no matter how you figured trouble, there was no doubt this time. He was in some shit. And not like that morning on deck. This time *he* was the lost plane, spiraling and smoking. Oren downshifted. The Merc's cockeyed headlight beams met and crossed ahead. On either side, the dark trees leaned over the narrow road and the headlights made it seem like a pine tunnel. Wasn't much farther, Oren thought. Flett would be there already, fixing things. He hoped.

"Dad?"

Oren glanced at the kid, whose feet dangled over the edge of the bench seat and the scratchy Indian blanket he'd put there to keep the springs from popping through the torn upholstery. Michael was six, middle of three, only boy, and the only kid Oren got in the divorce. It had been his lawyer's advice: if he didn't want to pay so much, he needed to take a kid. So he got the boy. "Yeah?"

The kid's head was tilted to the side. "Do we live in water?"

Oren dragged his cigarette. "What?"

"Do we live in water?"

"What do you mean?"

"Do we live in water?"

"I don't . . . I don't know what you mean."

"I mean do we live in water?"

"You mean like in the rain or something? In the ocean?"

The boy stared at him.

"I don't . . ." Oren took a pull on the beer. "Do you mean *can* we live in water?"

"No. *Do* we live in water?"

The clearing had snuck up on Oren and he slowed, came into the cross of narrow country roads, nothing but dark walls of trees in four directions, and Flett's roadhouse in the center of this clearing, the big one story, low-slung building with no windows and a stumpy sign that read: TWO BRIDGES. A single lightbulb pointed back at the sign, night bugs frantic in the dim light. Oren pulled the Merc into the parking lot, the cackle of rubber on gravel.

He took a breath. "Listen. I gotta run in this place for a minute."

There were five other cars parked outside, including Flett's Chevy and that bitch of a red Cadillac that Ralph Bannen drove. Okay. Flett must be in there trying to smooth things with Bannen, working out some kind of arrangement. Earlier that day, Oren and the kid had driven out to Flett's new house overlooking the lake, and while the kid hung out in Flett's basement, Oren had explained how bad he'd messed up, how he'd been nailing this guy's whore of a wife, and how once on a drunk she happened to mention that her husband had a safe in the house. Oren guessed right off the wife's birth date as the combination. He'd only taken a little money, but the guy apparently counted every night and hit it out of the wife that Oren had been over. The whole time Oren told this story, Flett just stared, until he finally said, *What guy, Oren?* And when Oren told him Ralph Bannen, Flett just shook his head. Bannen ran book and women at half the clubs in the panhandle, including Two Bridges. After yelling at him, Flett had suggested going alone to the roadhouse, talking to Bannen, and then having Oren come down after he fixed things up. So Oren sat at Flett's house for an hour while the boy played in the basement. And now, here they were.

Oren dragged his smoke and stared at the kid again— blond like his mother, round-faced, big floppy eyelashes. He looked so much like her Oren wondered how he could like the kid so much.

"Sit tight," Oren said. "I gotta see this man. Don't get out of the car. You hear?"

The boy stared at him expectantly, as if waiting for the answer to a question, and that's when Oren remembered the boy had asked one. "Look, I don't know what you were talking about before, Michael," he said. "Do you mean can we breathe in water?"

"No," the boy said, as plainly as if he were asking for a sandwich. "Do. We. Live. In water?"

Oren pulled smoke again. And then he surprised himself by laughing.

1992

THE NUMBERS clicked to a stop, the tank full, and Michael replaced the nozzle and screwed the gas cap back on the rental. He craved a cigarette. It was all he could do to not go into the convenience store and buy a pack. Two years and still . . . maybe he'd just feel this need forever. He started the car and pulled back onto the highway, shocks hunching up on the blacktop. It was more developed out here than he'd imagined, businesses all along this stretch, the grubby outskirts of a resort community: tavern, little grocery, machine shop, Western boot store, sawmill, wrecking yard, and a couple of nicer mobile home parks. From the news story, he'd imagined it more remote than this, forested and dark, not a civilized string of small businesses.

Locals called the area Two Bridges, this unincorporated strip of businesses connecting the northern and eastern shores of the lake—overgrown with restaurants and tourist stores, and on the busiest corners, the place Michael had come to see, the oldest thing in the area: Two Bridges Restaurant and Resort.

The resort was comprised of three newer buildings: a Western-themed restaurant and lounge in front, with faux wagon-wheel windows; a General Store that sold driftwood and Indian art; and the hotel out back, a big eight-story Vegas-style tri-sided structure with a sign promising, "Lake views!"

Michael got out of the car, grabbed his briefcase, and walked past the restaurant down a sidewalk, between land-scaped strips of grass, toward the front door of the motel. The desk clerk showed him into an office overlooking the hotel lobby, on a mezzanine directly above the front desk. A few minutes later a woman came into the room, mid-thirties, short and plump with dark hair and a round bosom and in-troduced herself as Ellie Flett. It was the woman he'd talked to on the phone. "You're the lawyer from San Francisco who wanted to talk about his father?"

"Yes." He offered his hand. "Michael Pierce." And it oc-curred to him that he hadn't really thought about where to start, or for that matter, where to go once he'd started. He reached in his briefcase and pulled out a news story that a clip service had found for him in the Spokane newspaper, just over the border from the lake, a story published four years earlier: "Historic Two Bridges Resort to Expand." The story had been about the construction project, but it had referred to the resort's history as a roadhouse and home for gambling and prostitution before this side of the lake was developed. As he handed the story over, Michael saw that his hand was shaking.

Ellie Flett didn't seem to notice. She took the story and pointed over his shoulder to the same story, laminated and framed on the wall behind him with a handful of other clippings. Michael hadn't expected this to be so hard.

"My mother died two years ago," Michael said. "She raised my sisters and me. We never knew our father. It was something we never talked about. There were no pictures, nothing. She remarried when I was ten. A good man, my stepfather. Shane Pierce," he added, explaining his last name. And as true as all of this was, it seemed like something other than the point of this visit and he rubbed his brow, confused by the disconnect he felt from this seemingly intimate information. "After my mother died, my sister found this note in her things." Michael handed her a faded slip of yellow paper covered in small printed letters, as if a shy child had written the note.

Katie, Sorry I couldn't take the boy after all. I got in some trouble. Just like you said. He's a good boy. Tell him I said so. You tell him it's okay he can do anything he wants.
Oren.
    I'll come back when I can.

Ellie didn't look up from the note. "This was your father?"

"Oren Dessens," Michael said. She showed no reaction to the name.

Ellie turned the page over. Stamped in light blue ink on

the other side of the narrow strip of paper were the words TWO BRIDGES and, running down the left-hand column, the numbers one to fifteen.

"This is a betting slip," Ellie said. One corner of her mouth went up. "I used to see these around the house when I was a kid."

She stared at the slip like an old family picture. And then she laughed. "Back in the old days, before all the money flooded into the valley, they used to take sports betting out here. Games were written on a chalkboard and these numbers corresponded to each game on the board." Ellie smiled at the memory and then looked down at the betting slip. "'*I'll come back,*'" she read.

"'*When I can,*'" Michael finished the line.

"I guess he didn't."

"No," Michael said. There was some other part to all of this, something about his own divorce, but Michael didn't know how to tell that part. "I was surprised about my father saying he couldn't take me after all," he said instead. "My mom never mentioned me living with him. Shane, my stepfather, said the only thing my mother ever said about Oren was that he was a gambler and a drunk who took off for good when I was six. She heard he put out on a ship and figured he died of syphilis somewhere."

Ellie was staring at him in a way that made Michael feel exposed.

"But," Michael said, "naturally, when I found the story about this place . . ." He didn't finish, and wondered, naturally . . . what? Did he expect to find his father here?

Ellie looked back at the betting slip. "Look. I've got a meeting I can't miss. A convention we're trying to get. But . . . do you want to talk to my dad?"

"Your dad?"

"Tim Flett. He bought the place in the fifties from the original owner, probably about the time you're talking about. He's not in the best of health, but his mind is still sharp. Maybe he remembers your father."

They made an appointment to meet again in an hour. Michael left her office, took an elevator to the eighth floor of the hotel, and stood in the hallway looking out. From the top floor, he could see the lake in the distance and the two highways parting ways at a 90-degree angle from one another, skirting the shores of the lake and disappearing in a blur of commercial development.

Again, it wasn't the way he'd pictured it, and it seemed odd to him that he'd pictured anything at all. Maybe it was the news story, which made reference to the dark history of the place: the Western toughs, the gamblers and hookers. And Oren's note: *I got into some trouble*. Was this enough to fuel his imagination? And what about the other things he saw, the cowboy boots and Indian blankets, the bright shimmering wall?

On the top floor, Michael found he had cell phone coverage again, and he listened to a new message from Tracy: "I know you're up in Idaho. I just wanted to tell you that I'm leaving Megan's Babysitter Club books on the built-in in the living room." And then she paused. "She's worried about having something to read when she comes to your house." The words *your house* were a kick to Michael's stomach. He could tell Tracy felt it too. On the message, she sounded clipped, holding something back. "I hope you find what you're looking for, Michael."

He pressed the button to delete the message, but as her

voice faded, Tracy said, "Oh, and one more . . ." but she was gone. He tried to call her and got no answer.

He met Ellie in the lobby. "You can ride with me," she said and started for the front door before he could answer. She wore a soft black leather coat, and as he followed her out to the parking lot, Michael shifted uneasily. After the years of cheating on Tracy, maybe it was just muscle memory with him, the guilt.

"This whole area is different from how it was thirty years ago," Ellie said as they drove away from the resort. "There were only two cabins on this whole side of the lake when I was born. Now, they're like tract homes. Seccondaries a mile from the lake go for four hundred thousand. Our little crop-duster airport is full of private jets." She said a couple of celebrities' names, conspiratorially, the same names that Michael had read about in his research, almost as if the names themselves had become tourist attractions.

They drove away from the crossroads, down the southbound four-lane highway, past an Indian casino, its parking lot jammed with cars. "This side of the lake was all forest back then," she said. "It was the untamed side." Michael thought about telling her that he'd pictured it that way. But what would be the point? "My dad tells some pretty wild stories," she said. "Crazy how much can change in thirty years."

He'd had that thought recently, too—how far removed he felt from a father who fought in World War II and gambled at roadhouses. "I remember driving from Tahoe one time," Michael said, "and going through the Donner Pass and thinking that just a few generations before, that little spot was impassable, and turned people into animals. And now I can just . . . drive through it. Like any stretch of highway."

They drove a few more miles, and then cut along an access

road winding down a hillside above the shoreline. Ellie drove slowly past cute signs with nautical themes and stacked mailboxes above clusters of cabins and A-frames.

"My dad built the first cabin on this side, in fifty-five," Ellie said. She turned off the road and they came around a huge boulder to the back of a modest, wood-frame building with windows facing the lake and stairs down to the rocky shore. Michael had the strange sensation of seeing what he'd imagined. "Thank you for doing this," he said.

Ellie turned off the car and stared at the house. "That time of my father's life fascinates me," she said. "It's hard to reconcile the stories he tells with the sweet, silly man he is now." She opened her door and paused. "Oh. Before we go in . . . there's something you should know about my dad. It can be jarring if you're not prepared for it."

1958

BANNEN SLAPPED him like he was a damn woman. Oren Dessens spun and fell against the craps table, cheek stinging. He scurried backward, beneath the table, and against the scratchy cedar wall. He put his hands up as Bannen stalked toward him. "Wait, wait. Just listen to me—"

"Oh. He wants me to listen." Bannen spoke over his shoulder, to nervous hacks of laughter. The place was nearly empty, just the handful of Bannen's usual ass-sniffers, tough guys as long as they were together. It was dark, all the lights shut off except the one behind the bar. Bannen's thick jaw was clenched and his white hair had come out of its straight furrows and was falling down in his eyes. "You believe this guy? Steals from me and now he wants me to listen to him. You believe this son-of-a-bitch?"

Oren looked up at Flett, standing beside the craps table, his shoulders turned a few degrees. He was fingering some chips and staring at his shoes. Oren had foolishly believed that Flett could run interference for him, plead his case to Ralph Bannen. Now Oren saw there was no way Flett could do that. And he didn't really blame him. Flett was in no position to get him a deal. He owned the roadhouse but it was Bannen who ran book out of it and who paid off the sheriff, Bannen who brought the whores up from Wallace and who muscled the guys who couldn't pay. Oren had thought he was pleading his case to the house by going to Flett, but Bannen had always been the house. And it was Bannen's ex-whore wife he'd banged, and Bannen's safe he'd broken into. He remembered something that Flett always said: only three kinds of trouble out here—money, women, and Ralph Bannen. I hit the trifecta, Oren thought.

He started to pull himself up against the cedar wall and felt a sharp kick to his side that lifted him and dropped him to the floor again. A cowboy boot. Oren thought it might have split his ribs. When he could open his eyes, he looked up to the pinched face of Rutledge. Rutledge, who he'd run down to Lewiston not three weeks ago to fish steelhead. Jesus. This was bad. The guys, five of them including Bannen and Flett, stood circled around him, a pack of dogs. Oren wheezed.

"So what do I do?" Bannen asked. He looked around the circle, grim male faces all of them, eyes darkened by the dim lights in this room, all of them with shadowy evening beards. "What about you, Timmy? What would you do with a guy like this?"

Tim Flett was Oren's age, thirty-three, their birthdays just two months apart. Oren wondered why this would come to him now, maybe because it was the only thing. Otherwise, they couldn't be more different. Tim was a local, grew up in his daddy's sawmill and lived a mile from where he was born. Oren was a roamer from Montana originally, who'd skipped along the Highline after the war, then down into the Idaho panhandle and into Washington. Tim was a settler, took the money he inherited from his old man, bought this roadhouse and built his home on the lake. Oren couldn't settle for anything, even a perfectly good girl like Katie. Always scratching for money, losing jobs, chasing trouble. Oren wondered if he could've been a guy like Tim Flett, living above the surface, instead of always below.

"Shoot, Ralph. I don't know," Flett said. He was a pretty big guy himself, with short red hair curled tight on top and cheeks and neck that were always scarlet. But he wasn't *big* like Bannen, whose chest heaved in and out as he breathed.

"No. Come on, Timmy. Tell me." Bannen looked around. "This is your place. What would you do to a guy who dicks your wife so he can steal from you?"

Oren didn't dare correct him. Bannen's wife had been one of the sweeter whores Bannen ran before he took her out of commission, and getting *her* had always been the point. The safe was an afterthought. No, he'd only taken a little of Bannen's money, but he'd had every last bit of the man's wife.

Flett made eye contact with Oren and then looked away. "Since he came in on his own, I'd just hit him around some," Flett said quietly, "maybe break something." He looked at Oren again, and seemed to want him to know this was the best he could possibly do. "And then he's gotta get so far outta town that not only do you never see him again, you never hear his name again."

So that was the play. It was, Oren saw, as much defense as Flett could offer on his behalf. And at that moment, sucking air through the pain of broken ribs, his face burning, staring up at Ralph Bannen, Oren was grateful for it.

"I don't know," Bannen said, way too quickly, and Oren went cold. "I don't think that'll do it for me, Timmy. I know this piece of shit is your friend, but that just . . . just don't do it for me."

That was when Oren moved. He moved like he moved in poker, not thinking about it until he did it, the way he never looked at his cards until it was his bet, because if *he* had no idea what he had, then no one else would be able to read him. He jumped, grabbed hold of the leg of the craps table, and pulled it over between him and Bannen. And then he had to find a spot through the semicircle. Flett, of course. It was the only play and Flett seemed to know it. Oren hit his friend full in the chest with his shoulder and the man gave, stumbled backward into a blackjack table behind him. Rutledge grabbed for him but Oren spun and was out the door. It was cold outside. He'd come out the back door, opposite side of the parking lot, and he ran as fast and as low as he could, into the trees. At first he couldn't tell if anyone was behind him, but then he could hear voices and the crunch of brush.

Oren ran like an animal, scrambling and darting, almost on all fours. The air burned his lungs. He tripped over something and scratched himself but he barely slowed. Tree limbs swatted at him. It was so dark in these woods that, when his eyes finally adjusted, he found it nearly impossible to believe he hadn't run full into a tree. They were thick all around him and he moved like a kid running through a crowd of—Oh, shit.

Oren came to a stop, panting.

Goddamn it! He looked back over his shoulder. He'd brought Michael to Flett's house earlier in the day, that was one thing. But bringing a six-year-old to Two Bridges—what was he thinking? He wasn't, that's what. He could've easily taken the kid to Katie's for the night. Flett had even suggested leaving Michael at his house, in the basement. "You see how much he loves them fish," Flett had said. "He'll be fine."

Maybe Flett would find the kid and take him home. Even Bannen, asshole that he was, wouldn't take out adult business on a kid. Would he? Oren needed to keep moving. Make his way south, to the highway, to Hayden. Maybe boost a car.

He started running again but the adrenaline was fading and his broken rib cut him with each inhale. He saw a crease in the hillside and could hear water trickling. He ran down and found an old logging road hacked into the forest, two lines of faint tire tracks. Where the road crossed the creek they'd put in a culvert, a round section of corrugated no bigger than a man could crawl through. Oren dropped down to the creek bed, just above the water line, and ducked into it. There was just a trickle of water. He could stay here till morning. He thought about his escape and felt a sort of pride. It seemed big to him, epic, the kind of story men would repeat through the ages. He'd nailed Bannen's wife and got away with it. That kind of story attached itself to a man forever. That is, if anyone ever found out about it. It was black dark. Oren closed his eyes.

He pictured the boy sitting in the car again. Don't move, he had told the kid when he went inside to straighten things out. And the kid wouldn't move. Oren had only had Michael for three months, since the divorce went final, but he was a good kid. He did what he was told, and most of the time he sat in the apartment Oren rented in Coeur d'Alene, staring out at the traffic on the street like it was a damn television. Shit, the kid might sit in that car forever. What was the crazy question he'd asked on the way out here from Flett's house? Water. Oren laughed to himself as he crouched in the culvert, icy creek flowing around the rubber of his boots.

So, what if Flett didn't find the boy in the car? What if they spent all night looking for Oren? Michael would sit there all night. It was cold out here. What if Michael came looking for him? He pictured Bannen grabbing his kid and Oren felt something hot rise in his throat. Maybe Bannen *would* take it out on the boy. Or just hold him somewhere until Oren showed up.

He couldn't stop his thoughts, which were like another broken rib.

They'd never expect him to go back. He told himself this, but it was stupid justification.

He wasn't going back because it was the smart play.

He was going back because of the boy.

Son of a bitch, this makes no sense, Oren thought, as he edged himself out of the culvert, thinking of that Japanese plane again, and the way it just fell out of the sky.

1992

TIM FLETT lay like a stranded whale on a massive brown leather couch, in a room overlooking the lake, watching a big screen television that had been planted in front of the fireplace mantel. It was hard to see where the couch ended and where the old widower began. He was, as his daughter Ellie had explained outside, a mess—the result of runaway diabetes and a strep infection that had almost killed him. He was missing his left leg to the knee and his right foot, parts of three fingers on his left hand, and he was wearing an eye patch over his left eye, beneath thick glasses. But that was not to say there wasn't a lot of Tim Flett: massive, great foothills of haunches rising into a rolling stomach covered with big gray sweats and bare arms dimpled and pinched beneath gray sheets of skin, rising to the thick red folds of his neck and chest. He breathed like two men snoring. His hair was red, short and curly, and it was hard to tell it from the mottled skin on his neck and head. He looked up from the TV and smiled.

"Hiya, sweetheart," he said to his daughter.

Ellie introduced Michael, who looked around the cabin's main room. Three big windows looked out on the bay. The walls were cut from halved logs and the room was rustic, like a small lodge, with stuffed fish and family pictures competing for wall space. Next to the couch was a big, solid-looking portable toilet, on the other side of it a dormitory refrigerator.

"Forgive my appearance," Tim Flett said. "I'm donatin' my body to science. One piece at a time."

Ellie smiled. Michael wondered how many times she'd heard that joke.

"Did the nurse come by this afternoon, Dad?"

"She's a nurse?" Tim Flett asked, looking at Michael for a reaction. "Well, that explains it. I thought she was just a really clean hooker."

When Flett was done laughing and there was a lull, Michael reached in his briefcase for the news story and the betting slip. Ellie watched him. "Dad," she said, leaning forward. "Michael is trying to find out about his father." And then she told the story: how Michael's mother had died a year earlier, that he was the middle of three kids, even his father's name. "Did you know this man, Oren Dessens?"

Tim Flett's eyes shot to Michael's. And the hand with the missing fingers seemed to rise of its own accord to rub the big man's jaw. "You're Oren's boy?" He looked past Michael, out the window to the lake. "Christ. I can't believe it. Oren Dessen's boy."

Michael rose and handed him the betting slip. Flett took it with his good hand, which shook with the effort. "I ain't seen one of these in . . ." He trailed off, turned it over and read the note. "Jesus," he said. He looked at Michael again. "Oren Dessens. Jesus. I can't believe you're here."

"Do you know what happened to him?" Michael asked.

Flett looked up, his eyes wet. "Not really," he answered after a long pause. "Not after he left here. There was some trouble. The night he wrote this." His skin reddened. "Oren took some money from this woman and her husband. He came out here to have me straighten it out, but the guy he owed the money to was a hard guy." He looked at Ellie. "I ever tell you about Ralph Bannen, honey?"

Ellie shook her head. "I don't think so."

"Big old guy. Bigger'n me even. His back looked like a damn barn. Last time I saw your dad," Flett said, "was that night. Bannen wasn't the kind of guy you could stay in town if you'd screwed him." Flett stared out at the lake. "He run your dad off."

"This guy my father owed money to," Michael said, "is he still alive?"

"Ralph?" Flett frowned. "No. Bannen's wife fixed him with his own baseball bat not long after, maybe six months. SOB bled to death. Took him all night to die. He'd been

pounding on her for years. She only did two years for club-
bing him, even though she hit him four times and didn't call
nobody for hours. Jesus, he was a big man. I'm surprised it
didn't take ten hits with that bat."

"And my father. Do you know where he went?"

Flett was staring out at the lake, smiling, and at first Michael didn't think he'd heard the question. But he cleared
his throat and answered. "He said he was going to Seattle to
catch a boat. Merchant Marine."

And then Flett smiled. "Your father used to talk about
the places he saw in the navy. Islands. Australia and I don't
know. Samoa. I'd never been nowhere but Washington and
Montana, so your dad might as well have been talking about
Mars. But after he left, I always pictured him living on one
of them islands, sleeping with the dark girls and cheating the
locals at poker."

They talked a little more, but Flett didn't seem to remember anything else. When it was quiet, Ellie offered to show
Michael around. They walked outside and down the exterior
wooden staircase, the rail in bad need of stain. The water
lapped silently against the rip-rap and a dock lifted and fell
slightly.

"I'm sorry he couldn't help you more," Ellie said.

"It's okay," Michael said. "At least he knew him."

"What will you do now?"

"I guess I'll go to Seattle, see if they keep Merchant Marine
records there."

Ellie was staring at him. "Can I ask you something?"

Michael said yes.

"You said you've been looking for your father the last four
months."

"Yes."

"But you said your mother died a year ago. So what happened four months ago?"

Michael looked down and smiled. "My wife and I split."

After a moment, Ellie said, "I'm sorry."

Michael shrugged. That was such an odd phrase—*My wife and I split*—so matter-of-fact and impermanent, making it sound no different than *My wife and I bought a home* or *My wife and I joined a softball team*. So what was the truth? That he threw his life away? That he self-destructed and threw away the whole goddamn thing? That his daughter was worried about having books to read at his house? Michael stared at his hands. "A hole opened up."

"What?" she asked.

He was surprised that he'd spoken. "Nothing," he said. But he finished the thought: A hole opened up and he had to know what was inside it. So he picked and picked until the hole was huge, and then everything sort of . . . fell in, him, his wife, his kid, and this fragile life they'd built at the edge of the hole. And that's why he was here, because he'd begun wondering if maybe his father hadn't fallen in the same hole—

Chop rolled over the surface of the lake.

Michael looked down the shoreline, at nodding docks, at ski boats rising and falling against log pilings. "It's nice up here," he said.

"It's quiet," she said, as if that was the same thing.

They went back in the house through the basement and were starting up the stairs when something caught Michael's eye in a room just off the stairs. He pushed open the door to a small bedroom. An empty fish tank ran the length of one wall, a big aquarium eight feet long, like a coffin. The water had been drained and all that was in the tank was a wire brush, a pump, some fake seaweed and a little ceramic turtle. Michael stood at the door a moment and then stepped into the room, empty except for a bed, a dresser, and this wall-length fish tank. He reached up and put his hand against the cold glass.

"This was my room when I was a kid," Ellie said, looking around.

"There were lights," Michael said quietly, his hand against the glass.

"In the tank? Yeah."

"Blue lights," he said.

"My dad put the tank in before I was born. He loved fish." She laughed. "I always thought the lights made the fish look like ghosts, but I didn't have the heart to tell him how much this tank scared me. You must have had one, too."

A fading current seemed to connect Michael to the glass, a dying memory, dissolving in the very moment he remembered it, like a dream he woke to, trying to recount in the morning as it faded (*fish gliding in the blue* . . .).

Then it was gone, whatever it had been—daydream, memory, trick of the mind—and Michael Pierce let his hand fall from the glass. He remembered Tracy saying in her message that Megan had left some books on a shelf, and at that moment all he wanted to do was go home and run his hand over the spines of those little books.

"No," he said to Ellie. "I didn't have one of these."

They went back upstairs. Tim Flett was working the remote control, running through channels on the television. He didn't look up.

Michael put his card on the little end table next to the old man. "If you happen to remember anything more about my father."

"I said. He put out on a boat in Seattle."

"No, I'm just saying . . . if you remember anything else—"

Tim Flett's eyes shot from the TV to Michael to the window. "I told you," he said sharply. "He put out on a goddamn boat!"

"Dad!" Ellie scolded. And then to Michael: "I'm sorry. He's tired."

"It's okay," Michael said. He followed the old man's eyes to the window, and beyond that, the dark, still lake. Whole worlds exist beneath the surface. And maybe you can't see down there, Michael thought, but there's a part of you that knows.

1958

THEY RODE silently toward Flett's house. Bannen drove his Caddy, alone in the front seat. Oren sat in back, trying not to breathe too deeply. Sitting on either side of him were Rutledge and the other man, Baker, whom he barely knew.

The road to Flett's cabin was barely more than tire tracks in the trees. They came to the house, lights on, casting white tips on the surface of the lake.

Oren had run into the three men on his way back to the roadhouse, stepping out of the trees with his hands up, pleading with them, explaining that his kid was in the car. Bannen told him that Flett had already taken his kid back to the lake house, and it came to Oren that he could've just stayed in the woods. They hit him around a little more and then dragged him back to the car.

Baker and Rutledge pulled Oren out of the car by the arms. His head hung to his chest.

Flett came out of the house, looking concerned. He wouldn't meet Oren's eyes.

"Where's Michael?" Oren asked.

"Downstairs," Flett said, without looking at him. "He's fine."

"Look. I need you to take him home, Tim," Oren said. "Take him to Katie's. Will you do that for me?"

"Oren," Flett began.

"Come on. I don't want him to see this."

Flett considered the request. He pulled Bannen over to the edge of the house, beneath the porch light, and turned so that his back was to Oren. He spoke quickly, gesturing with his hands. Bannen just seemed to listen.

"I know I got a beating coming," Oren said quietly to Rutlege and Baker, who held his arms. "But don't let him kill me. Okay? I mean . . . if it starts to look bad—"

But he didn't finish and they didn't say anything. Oren took a deep breath and it felt like another kick in his side. "Christ. Do you sharpen them boots, Rutledge?"

"Sorry, Oren," he said.

Bannen and Flett came back. "You got two minutes with the kid," Bannen said.

Oren, with Baker and Rutledge still on his arms, followed Flett into the house and down the stairs, into the bedroom on the right. And there was the boy, staring into Flett's giant aquarium, tropical fish swimming around in the blue light, a big square-headed whiskered thing probing the glass, and a skinny one with streaks of gold and a flitty little yellow one that darted in among the phony rocks. Michael was so close his nose almost touched the glass and his face was as blue as the fish, as he watched them swim the way he watched traffic out the window of Oren's apartment, the way he looked at Oren in the car, the way he looked out at the world. And that's when Oren understood.

Do we live in water?

He watched the fish come to the end of its blue world, invisible and impassible, turn, go around and turn again as he sensed another wall and another and on and on. It didn't even look like water in there, so clear and blue. And the goddamn fish just swam in its circles, as if he believed that, one of these times, the glass wouldn't be there and he would just sail off, into the open.

Oren put his hand on the kid's shoulder.

Michael turned.

"We ain't like fish, Michael," Oren said. "You can do whatever you want."

The kid looked back at the tank.

Oren turned to Flett. His throat felt tight. "Will you take Katie a note?"

Flett nodded and handed him a betting slip and a pen. Oren concentrated on the note. He wrote carefully. He signed his name, and then thought of one more thing to say. "I'll come back when I can." It gave him a kind of courage. He finished the note and handed it to Flett, who wouldn't meet his eyes.

"Listen," Oren said to Flett, "if this goes bad, I got a boat in Seattle."

"Oren," Flett said. "If there was anything I could . . ."

"No. Listen to me," Oren said, his voice cracking. "I'm goin' on a boat. Anyone asks. I got a boat in Seattle. Okay?"

Finally, Flett nodded.

They moved back up the stairs, Flett and the boy first, and him and Baker and Rutledge behind. If he was going to run again, this was probably his best bet. But Oren knew he needed to see the boy get in that car first.

Bannen was smoking. God he wanted that cigarette. But Bannen just dropped it when Oren came out. Flett opened the passenger door to the Chevy and the boy climbed in. He looked out the window at Oren, gave a little wave. Oren's chin quivered but he felt brave again, as if Bannen couldn't touch him. Oren waved back, the guys standing close to him, but not holding his arms, trying to make it seem casual.

He watched Flett's car back up, turn and head down the road. The hands gripped Oren's arms again and Bannen went to the trunk of his car. When the big man returned with a bat, Oren's head fell to his chest. He strained then, but he knew.

Rutledge and Baker tightened their grip and Oren's feet scratched at the dirt driveway. He could just see dawn start to break on the foothills above the lake but Bannen wasn't likely to wait. The first swing took him in the lower back and folded him. Oren lost whatever breath he'd had and felt something give in his hip. The hands let go of him and he dropped to the ground, pawing for his breath. He closed his eyes and tried to find something to look at in his mind. He came back to that morning on the carrier, the blue sky and the ocean, and where they met, that endless line. Everything that isn't sky and water lives for a moment in that little gray band. Above and below it, the blue stretches forever.

THIEF

IT'S GOT TO BE the girl.

Wayne opens her door and hall light spills over the bedroom floor, across her sleeping face. She's fourteen. Sits all day in headphones, glares out at the world. Wears her jeans too tight. Pretends to walk to the bus stop and gets in that knucklehead's Nova. Tapes album covers all over walls—like this jackass guitar player with curly hair above her bed: FRAMPTON COMES ALIVE! On the pillow, her hair looks like Frampton's—a ratty halo. She spends thirty minutes on it every morning, runs up half the power bill on the goddamn blow dryer. Wayne looks at the other albums on the wall. What the hell is a blue oyster cult? She's probably smoking pot.

But a thief?

Asleep she looks like she's never had a bad thought in her life.

She was the first, when Wayne was still in the navy. Closed her tiny red hand around his pinky and Wayne thought: *What the hell have I done?* That tightness in his chest. He was nineteen. Only five years older than she is now. Last summer someone stole a few of his Pall Malls, and although he never caught her with the smokes, she was his prime suspect then, too.

Wayne eases the door closed, steps down the hall to the boys' room. Little and Middle, nine and eleven, splayed on twin beds like they were dropped fifty feet. The Little one could be it out of temperament alone. He's a hoarder, a brooder. Dark eyes like his mother. Looks up from his Legos like you interrupted church. Kid didn't say a word until he was four and then it was a full sentence: "I want more applesauce now." Acts like he's never had an entire meal. Pockets food during dinner, squirrels Halloween candy in dresser drawers, carries acorns around in his mouth. By personality, it could be the Little one. He's got that want thing in his eyes. The want Wayne sometimes gets.

On the top bunk, the Middle one mutters in his sleep. Milkman's kid, Wayne always joked, not just because he's blond, but because he's so different from Wayne. He hates to say it about his own kid, but the Middle one's a pussy. Falls down and gets hurt, wrecks his bike and cries and pisses his pants (at eleven?), plays chess and always has his head in a book and can't seem to keep his goddamn finger out of his nose. "Hey," he told the boy one time, "when you finally get whatever's up there, let me know. I want to see it." The kid just stared at him. The Middle one could be it just because Wayne has no idea what goes on in that head of his. He's an alien.

"Wayne?"

Karen stands behind him in the hallway, white nightie, dark eyes squinting.

"Hey baby."

"It's two in the morning."

"Yeah, Ken and I had a couple after work."

"Come to bed."

"Did I ever tell you about our trip to Yellowstone when I was a kid? We stayed in these cabins at this Indian camp, least that's what they called it. There was a creek to pan for gold and a field of arrowheads. My sister told me the gold and arrowheads were fake, that the people who ran the roadside deal planted them for us to find." Wayne smiles at the memory. "My dad had to park on a hill every night to compression-start that old Ford of his. Imagine. My cranky old man driving around flat eastern Montana looking for a hill to park on." But he can't remember why he brought it up.

"Just come to bed."

Wayne sighs and looks back at the boys. He'd have to go long odds on the Middle kid, six-to-one, out of ineptness alone, two-to-one on the Little boy, because of his sneaky personality. Even money on the Girl . . . just because.

In the bedroom, Karen turns her tapered back to him, the straps of her nightgown just above the waterline of covers. Wayne takes his change out of his pockets. Two quarters, a dime, four pennies.

Okay. Here we go. Every night after work, after the tavern, he drops his change in the Vacation Fund on their closet floor. The Vacation Fund is a gallon glass jar, a replica of an old rotgut whiskey jar, dark brown glass, wide at the bottom, narrow as a fifty-cent piece at the neck, with a glass finger-handle at the very top. When the jar is full, the family has enough money to take a vacation. Just like Wayne's dad used to do it. Takes two years to fill the jar, two years to save enough for a summer car trip.

When Wayne noticed that someone was stealing from the Vacation Fund, he started leaving traps. He'd tilt the jar till the change ran uphill, then come home and find the sea of coins flat. Or he'd turn the handle to six o'clock, come home and find the handle at four-thirty, the jar moved off its indentation in the carpet. He even marked quarters, left them on top, and sure enough, the marked quarters disappeared.

Wayne gets down to eye level. The handle's turned to eight o'clock.

"I'll be goddamned!" He hoists the heavy jar and holds it up to the light. Two days this week; the thief is getting brash.

"Please, Wayne," Karen says from the bed. "You're imagining the whole thing."

"I'm imagining at least four bucks missing?"

"Four dollars? From a jar of two hundred?"

"It ain't the money, Karen. This is our vacation. You want one of your kids stealing from their own goddamn family? You want your kids to do this? To *be* like this?"

"Come to bed."

Wayne's hands are shaking. One of *his* kids. Christ.

"NO WAY," Ken says.

"Then who? Karen?"

"No. Course not."

"You think some cat burglar's breaking into my house to steal a few quarters at a time?"

"No. But your kids? Your kids are good fucking kids, Wayne."

His kids *are* good kids. Get A's. Polite. *Not* shitheads. Wayne presses his arms against the worn padding of the bar.

The door behind them opens and it's that Donna, tart secretary from the Union Hall. She walks the length of the bar, sings hi to everyone. Then she and Ken go through the whole thing of pretending they're not screwing. "It's the Ken and Wayne show. What are you fellas up to?"

"Hey Donna," Ken says. "How you been?" Like he didn't poke her in his car just last night.

It's only his second beer but Wayne wants out of there. His watch says 11:50. Someone has put goddamn Anne Murray on the jukebox. Pool balls clatter. Wayne bangs his glass on the bar. "Well. I should——"

"Nah, stay, man," Ken says, half-assed. Wayne doesn't blame Ken. After a night on the pot-line, breathing that slag steam, who wouldn't want a knock at Donna? Wayne likes to think that if she ever came at him, he'd say no—she ain't half as good-looking as Karen—but part of him thinks he couldn't say no. Shit. Sometimes he hates people.

"Yeah, stay for one more, Wayne," Donna says, less half-assed than Ken did. She puts a hand on his arm.

But tomorrow's Friday and Wayne's got one last swing on the pot-line before a three-day and then he rotates to a week of day shifts. He puts his coat on. "Nah, I'm goin' home. Gotta catch me a thief."

"A what?" Donna twirls her wedding ring.

Ken says, "One of Wayne's kids is stealing from his vacation fund."

"Where you going?" Donna asks.

"Kelowna," Wayne says. "B.C. That Fred Flintstone Land." And then he thinks of something—the thief started *after* Wayne picked that place. He thinks of the girl again. What fourteen-year-old wants to see Fred Flintstone Land?

Donna reaches for the beer Ken bought her. She's got on a tight silky dress with a red bow tied above her waist. "I hate kids," she says. "Especially mine."

THE MIDDLE one's finger is up to the first knuckle. His other hand holds his fork like a pencil.

"What do you think is up there?" Wayne asks. "A Three Musketeers?"

"Huh?" Middle kid always looks at him like he's just talked French.

"Don't do that at the table."

"Oh." The finger comes out of his nose like a sword from a scabbard. He straightens his glasses.

The Little boy smiles at his older brother's plight.

The Girl is a hundred miles away, herding stewed tomatoes.

"You ain't leaving the table until those tomatoes are gone."

"They're gross."

Karen tells how the Little one passed the Presidential Fitness.

"All except the pull-ups," he says, and shrugs. "Nobody could do the pull-ups so Mr. McAdam said to not worry about pull-ups."

Wayne looks at the Middle kid. He never passes the Presidential Fitness. Big crisis every year.

"I was in the sick room," he says. "I almost puked in science."

"Well, maybe next year," Wayne says.

The Middle one pushes his glasses up on his nose. He smiles wearily at his dad, as if to say, *Doubtful*.

"Can I go to Terry's after dinner?" the Girl asks, and she adds, "To do homework?"

"You bringing those tomatoes with you?"

The Girl slops a bite in her mouth.

Wayne stares at a bite of pork chop on his fork, at its perfect rind of pan-fried fat. "I've been thinking. About our vacation."

The kids all chew. Karen rolls her eyes and goes to get more rolls out of the oven.

"British Columbia still good with everyone?" He looks from kid to kid to kid. Before they can answer, he says, "Because it's not just Kelowna, you know. They got hot springs up there, and glacial lakes. And, uh, mountain goats."

The Little one pouts. "Wait. We're not going to Flintstone Land anymore?"

"No. Yeah. We're still going. I just mean we can go other places too."

"But how many days are we gonna be in Flintstone Land?"

"Vancouver would be cool."

"But at least two days, right?"

"Look, I don't know."

"There's a natural history museum in Vancouver."

"Vancouver's like a real city."

Wayne is sorry he brought it up. "Yeah, we'll see. Just finish your dinner."

Karen comes back in and gives them all a warm roll and him a cold look. She says, under her breath, "How'd it go, Detective?"

He glares at Karen, but the suspects don't seem to have heard her.

ON SUNDAY Wayne goes to the refrigerator. He gets two Lucky Lagers, puts them in the narrow closet, on the floor behind his four pairs of coveralls, which are hung behind his shirts. Then he opens the bathroom window. He goes back into his bedroom and grabs a clean set of coveralls from the closet. Glances down at the jar, makes sure the handle is straight up at midnight, and that it's precisely in its carpet indentation. He pulls the coveralls on over his jeans, up to his waist, the way he wears them when he's going to work. He starts down the hall.

He taps on the Girl's door, opens it and looks in. She's sitting cross-legged on her floor in front of her stereo. She sees him and takes off her headphones. "You gotta listen to this, Dad."

He comes in and puts the headphones on. It sounds just like all the other shit she listens to.

"Isn't that cool?"

Christ. "It's great," he says. He hands back the headphones.

"I thought you'd like it," the Girl says. "See, all my music isn't stupid."

"Hey," he says. "Your mom's helping Grandma Lil today and I got called in to work. You watch the boys a while?"

"Sure," she says, and puts the headphones back on. He leaves her door open.

The boys are playing army men. One takes the little green army, the other the little beige army. They spread the little plastic men on the floor across from each other and sit behind their armies throwing Legos at the other guy's army. First one to knock over all the other guy's army men wins. Moron game. They'll play this for hours, Karen finding the little plastic army men everywhere, behind couch cushions, in the laundry, under the table.

"Who's fighting?"

"I'm the Viet Cong," the Middle one says. "If you look at it a certain way, they're kind of like the American Revolutionaries."

Great. Middle one's a commie.

The Little one takes an army man out of his mouth. "I'm the Americans," he says proudly.

"Dad," the Middle one says, "you were in the navy after Korea but before Vietnam, right?"

"Right," Wayne says.

"So you didn't fight."

"No."

"I told you," the Middle one tells the Little one.

"But who were you versus?" the Little one asks.

"You ain't always versus someone. We just toured around the Pacific."

"Like a police car on patrol," Middle one says.

"Something like that."

"Huh," says Little one, and he puts the army man back in his mouth.

"Well, I'm headed in to work," Wayne says. "Your sister's in charge." The boys go back to playing and ignore him. "See you tonight."

Wayne goes outside. He climbs in his pickup truck. His day off and he's pretending to go to work. Karen's right; he is losing it. He knows Ken sometimes acts like he got called in, and then he goes and screws that Donna. Probably ball-deep in her right now. Shit, that almost makes more sense. He stares back at the house, a little one-story rambler. It's not that different from the house he grew up in. His old man was a welder, worked his ass off, sixty-hour weeks.

Wayne did it only once, stole from the Vacation Fund. He took two dimes. He was eight. Ed Hendry and his brother were going to the store. Wayne bought a pack of baseball cards and some stick candy with the stolen money. Worst fucking candy he ever ate. He'd thought, *Who's gonna miss two dimes?* But that whole trip, from Spokane to Yellowstone, he held his breath. *God, what if we run out of money?* He'd pray they found a hill to park on to start the car. *What if we run out of gas five miles from home and everyone turns to me? Look at that, Wayne. Two dimes short.*

Maybe Karen's right and this is all just guilt.

Wayne looks back at the house. But if he's right—and goddamn it, he wishes he wasn't, but he is—one of those shithead kids in there has stolen five or six times and keeps going back. That's what gets him. He did it once, and it almost killed him. You want your kids to do better than you did—his dad a welder, Wayne a good job at Kaiser Aluminum, maybe his kids will go to college. But you also want them to *be* better. And one of them is a goddamn thief? Christ. Wayne can't handle that. He's never hit his kids—a spanking here and there—but he's a little worried what he might do.

He starts his truck. Backs out of the driveway, takes one more glance at the house, drives down the street and parks at the grocery store on Trent. Slides out of his coveralls, leaves them in the truck, and humps home the two blocks. He goes through the back gate, to the side of the house, hoists himself up on the open windowsill, and eases down into the bathroom. He listens. It's quiet. Wayne takes off his boots, tiptoes through the bathroom, looks both ways, then slips into his and Karen's bedroom. He leaves the door open a bit. He creeps past the bed and into the closet.

There's the Vacation Fund, just inside the closet doorway, the jar set with the handle pointed straight up at midnight. Wayne steps past it, deeper into the closet. He slides behind his coveralls, which hang there like a curtain. He sits on the floor against the back wall, in the dark.

Wayne reaches for one of the beers, pops it, takes a drink. He'll sit here all day if he has to.

Maybe it is the Middle one. That shit about the Viet Cong? What was that?

He hears Karen again: *You're imagining things. You're losing it.*

Maybe. Wayne sits in the dark, drinking a cool Lucky Lager. He's not sure how much time passes. The caps have puzzles in them. The Girl and the Middle one race to solve them. Wayne pushes the coveralls aside to let some light spill into the back of the closet. He reads the bottle cap. A key. A chess pawn. A truck. The letters *ing.* Easy. *Key pawn truck ing*: keep on trucking.

Then he hears footsteps in the hall and lets the coveralls fall again, so he's in the dark. The bathroom door opens and then closes. Just someone going to the bathroom. He sighs, feels strangely relieved, and realizes how happy he'll be if he sits here all day, drinks these beers and nothing happens. If Karen's right. On the other side of the wall, the toilet flushes. Wayne takes a sip of his beer. More footsteps, soft on the carpet. Shit, the steps are coming this way. Wayne cocks his head to hear.

The floor creaks. One of them is inside the room. Wayne holds his breath. The steps come across the floor.

Then the closet door squeaks as someone opens it a little wider. Wayne covers his mouth. His older brother, Mike, was a thief. Stole from the neighbors. Stole a car once. Never amounted to shit. On his third divorce.

Wayne can hear breathing on the other side of the coveralls. He listens as the thief unscrews the lid of the jar. Goddamn it.

One of his kids! The thief tips the jar and some change comes out. Not much. Just a little. Wayne reaches out and puts his hand on the coveralls hanging in front of him. Karen has to wash them by hand, because of all the dirt and chemicals and shit. They're so heavy they'd screw up the washing machine.

The thief is going through the change. Dropping the pennies and nickels and dimes back in. Probably taking two or three quarters, just what Wayne would expect, just what he would do. Wayne counts to three. All he has to do is pull those coveralls aside.

He counts to three again. The thief screws the lid back on the jar.

The thief pushes the jar back into the closet. Wayne squeezes his eyes tight. *One of his kids is a sociopath. Now. Do it now. Caught you, you goddamn thief.*

But Wayne just sits curled up on the floor of his closet in the dark, behind his coveralls. He can't do it. He hears the feet pad across the room again. Out the door. Wayne's head falls to his knees. When it's quiet again, he reaches for the other beer.

The closet is three feet by five feet. The whole house is just nine hundred square feet. It's set on a fifty-by-sixty-foot plot of grass and dandelions, across from a vacant lot, in a neighborhood of postwar clapboards and cottages. The house cost $44,000. The interest rate is 13 percent. The father works rotating shifts at a dying aluminum plant—day, swing, graveyard—for $9.45 an hour, and he comes home so tired, so greasy, so black with soot and sweat that he's unrecognizable, and yet, every day he gets up to do it again. He sits in that closet with a beer, his head between his knees.

In the hallway, the thief burns with shame, the quarters two hot circles of mourning in my palm.

CAN A CORN

KEN TOOK dialysis Tuesdays and Thursdays. It fell to Tommy after his mom passed to check his stepdad out of the Pine Lodge Correctional Facility. Drop him at the hospital. Take him back three hours later.

Ken groaned as he climbed up the truck. —Whatcha got there, Tom?

Tommy looked over the back seat. —Pole and tackle.

—You goin' fishin' this weekend?

—I ain't skydivin'.

Ken stared out his window. —You stop me by a store?

There was a downtown grocery sold Lotto, fortified wines, and forties. Ken hopped out. Tommy spun radio stations until Ken came back with a can a corn.

—Oh, no you ain't, Ken.

—So got-damn tired, Tom. Can't sit on that blood machine today.

—You'd rather die?

—I'd rather fish.

—No way, Ken.

He drove toward Sacred Heart. But when Tommy stopped

at a red light Ken reached back, got the pole, and jumped out. Fine, Tommy thought. Die. I don't care. The old man walked toward the Spokane River. Tommy pulled up next to him, reached over, and popped the passenger door.

—Get in the damn truck, Ken.

Ken ignored him.

—That pole ain't even geared.

Ken walked, facing away.

Tommy drove alongside for another block. —Get in the truck, Ken.

Ken turned down a one-way. Tommy couldn't follow.

Fine. Stupid bastard. Tommy went back to work, but the only thing in the pit was a brake job on some old lady's Lincoln: six hundred in repairs on a shit-bucket worth three. Right. Pissed, Tommy gave the Lincoln to Miguel and drove back downtown.

He parked, got his tackle box from the truck, and walked back along the river. Found his stepfather under a bridge, dry pole next to him.

Tommy gave him hook and weight.

Ken's gray fingers shook.

—Give it here. Tommy weighted and hooked the line. He pulled a can opener from the tackle box and opened Ken's corn. Carefully, Tommy pushed the steel hook into the corn's paper skin until, with a tiny spurt, it gave way.

He handed the old man back the pole. Ken cast it.

Half-hour later, Ken reeled in a dull catfish, yellow-eyed and spiny. No fight in it. Almost like it didn't mind.

Ken held it up. —Well I will be got-damned.

Tommy released the fish. It just sort of sank.

He dropped the old man at the front gate of the prison, his

breathing already shallow. Rusty. He was so weak Tommy
had to reach over and pop his door again.

—Hey that wadn't a bad got-damn fish. All things considered. His eyes were filming over already. —We should go
again Tuesday.

—We gonna start playin' catch now, too? Tommy asked.

Ken laughed.

Tommy watched the old man pass through the metal gate.
The fucker.

VIRGO

YOU ALL SAY the same thing. You suits, you cops, you shrinks, you all sound alike: tell us what happened. Give us your side of the story. *My side* of the story. My side. As if truth were a box that you could flip over when you want another side, another version. Well, there are no sides, no box, maybe no truth.

You don't really want *my side* of the story. You don't want to understand me, know me, to crawl inside my head. You don't want to *feel* the things I've felt. You just want to know that one thing: why.

Fine. Here's why: Her. I did it all for her.

THIS ALL began in late October. We'd had the same old fight, with the same stale grievances Tanya had been lobbing at me for three months, almost since the day I moved in: *Blah, blah, stalled relationship; blah, blah, stunted growth; blah, blah, I worry that you're a psychopath.*

I said I'd try harder, but she was in a mood: "No, Trent. I want you out of here. Now." So I gathered my things. Four loads of clothes, shoes, CDs, action figures, and trading cards

I carried to my car. I was about to drive away when I saw . . . him. Mark Aikens, Tanya's missing-link ex-boyfriend, was loping up Twenty-first like some kind of predator, like a fat coyote talking on a cell phone. She had moved to Portland for this loser, even though she made twice as much as he did. She requested a transfer from the Palo Alto software company where she worked and found a small condo in the Pearl District, but she wasn't in town six months before he'd slept with someone else and she tossed him out. Mark Aikens was a cheating shit.

He swung around a light pole and skipped up the steps of our old building. She buzzed him up. Mark Aikens was a sous chef at Il Pattio, one of those jerkoffs who acts like cooking is an art. She always said he was sensitive, a good listener. Now he was up in our old condo, listening his sensitive, cheating ass off. For two hours I sat in my car down the block while this guy . . . listened. It grew dark outside. From the street, our condo glowed. I knew exactly which light was on—the up-right living room lamp. She got it at Pottery Barn. Through our old third-floor corner window I could see shadows move across the ceiling from that light and I tried to imagine what was happening by the subtle changes in cast: *She's going to the kitchen to get him a beer; he's going to the bathroom.* How many fall nights had I snuck home early from work and looked up to see the glow from that very light? It had been my comfort.

But now that light felt unbearably cold and far away, like an astronomer's faint discovery, a flicker from across the universe and the icy beginning of time. I might have gone crazy had I stared at that light much longer. In fact, I'd just decided to ring the buzzer and run when the unimaginable happened.

The light went out.

I sat there, breathless, waiting for Mark Aikens to come down. But he didn't. My eyes shot to the bedroom window. Also dark. That meant she was . . . they were . . .

I tooled around the Pearl having conversations with her in my head, begging, yelling, until finally I crossed the bridge and drove toward my father's little duplex in Northeast. I parked on the dirt strip in front and beat on his door. I could hear him clumping around inside. My dad had lost a leg to diabetes. It took him a while to get his prosthetic on.

When he finally answered, I said: "Tanya threw me out. She's seeing her old boyfriend. She said living with me was like living with a stalker."

"You always did make people nervous," my father said.

Dad was a big sloppy man, awful at giving advice. Since my mother's death, he'd been even less helpful in these father/son moments. He sniffed the air. "Have you been drinking?"

"No," I said.

"Christ, Trent." And he invited me inside. "Why the hell not?"

BEFORE ALL of this, I loved my job. And I'm not talking about the job as portrayed in my five-year-old performance evaluation, the low point of which (one flimsy charge of harassment stemming from an honest misunderstanding involving the women's restroom) the newspaper found a way to dredge up in its apology to readers. No. What I loved was the work.

As a features copy editor, I pulled national stories off the wire, proofread local copy, and wrote headlines for as many as five pages a day. My favorite, because it was Tanya's favorite, was "Inside Living"—page two of the features section, the best-read page in the *O*—with syndicated features like the crossword puzzle, the word jumble, celebrity birthdays, and Tanya's favorite, the daily horoscope. That's how we'd met, in fact, four months earlier, in a coffee shop where I saw her reading her horoscope. I launched our romance with a simple statement: "I edit that page." Within a week we were dating, and a month later, in late July, when I was asked to leave my apartment because the paranoid woman across the courtyard objected to my having a telescope, Tanya said I could move in with her until I found a place.

Now, to some, I may indeed be—as the newspaper's one-sided apology to readers characterized me—*strangely quiet and intense, practically a nonpresence*, but to loyal readers like Tanya, I was something of an unsung hero.

Each morning during those three glorious months, she would pour herself a cup of coffee, toast a bagel, and browse the newspaper, spending mere seconds on each page, until she arrived at "Inside Living," her newspaper home. I couldn't wait for her to get there. She'd make a careful fold and crease, set the page down, and study it as if it contained holy secrets.

And only then would she speak to me. "Eleven down: 'Film's blank Peak'?"

"Dante's."

"Are you sure you don't see the answers the day before?"

"I told you, no." Of course, I did see the answers the day before. But who could blame me for a little dishonesty? I was courting.

"Hey, it's Kirk Cameron's birthday. Guess how old he is."

"Twelve? Six hundred? Who's Kirk Cameron?"

"Come on. You edited this page yesterday. Now you're going to pretend you don't know who Kirk Cameron is?"

"That celebrity stuff comes in over the wire. I just shovel it in without reading it. You know I hate celebrities."

"I think you pretend not to like celebrities to make yourself appear smarter."

This was true. I do love celebrities.

"Hey, look," she'd say finally. "I'm having a five-star day. If I relax, the answers will all come to me."

It's painful now to recall those sweet mornings, the two of us bantering over our page of the newspaper, with no hint that it was about to end. And this is the strange part, the mystical part, some might say: on those days Tanya read that she was to have a five-star day . . . she actually had five-star days. Now, I don't believe in such mumbo-jumbo; it was likely just the power of suggestion. But I did begin to notice (in the journals in which I record such things) that Tanya was more open to my amorous advances when she got five stars. In fact, after our first month together, I began to notice that the only time Tanya seemed at all interested in being intimate, the only time she wanted to . . . you know, get busy . . . was when she got five stars on her horoscope.

Then one day in early October, when we'd stopped having sex altogether, I did it. I goosed her horoscope. Virgo was supposed to have three stars, and I changed it to five.

So sue me. It didn't even work.

OBVIOUSLY, THOUGH, that's where the idea came from. And yet I might have simply moved on after our breakup, and not launched my horoscope warfare, had Tanya not fired the first shot at me by filing a no-contact order a mere two weeks after throwing me out. A no-contact order! Based on what, I wanted to know.

"Well, you do drive over there every night after work and park outside her place," my dad said as he nursed a tumbler of rum.

"Yeah, but eight hundred feet? What kind of arbitrary number is that? Shall I carry a tape measure? How do you know if you're eight hundred feet away from someone? There's a tapas place around the corner from her condo. Am I just supposed to stop eating tapas?"

"There's a Taco Bell over on M.L. King."

"Tapas, Dad. Not tacos."

Dad poured us a drink, then turned on the TV. "Look, I don't know what to tell you, Trent. You make people uncomfortable. When you were a kid I thought something was wrong with your eyelids, the way you never blinked. I used to ask your mom if maybe there wasn't some surgery we could try."

This was my father. A woman breaks my heart and his answer is to sew my eyelids shut. But I suppose he tried. I suppose we all try.

"Life just isn't fair," I said as the old widower hobbled away on his prosthetic leg to get another drink.

"Yeah, well," he replied, "I hope I'm not the asshole who told you it would be."

The very next day, November 17, Virgo got the first of thirteen straight one-star days. *Four stars: your creativity surges. Keep an eye on the big picture,* Virgo was supposed to read that day. I changed it to: *"One star: watch your back."* It was glorious, imagining her reading that.

HOROSCOPES ARE cryptic and open-ended: *"You'll encounter an obstacle but you are up to the task. A Capricorn may help."*

In fact, I could argue that what clearly began as a way to spoil my girlfriend's day became a campaign to make horoscopes more useful. And I won't pretend that I didn't like the voice, the power that changing horoscopes gave me. In the office, I kept my own counsel, going days without speaking sometimes, but with these horoscopes I could finally say the things I'd been holding inside all those years. For our new drama critic, Sharon Gleason, I wrote, *"Libra. Three stars: those pants make you look fat."* For the arrogant sports columnist, Mike Dunne, *"Taurus. Two stars: I hope your wife's cheating on you."* For the icy young records clerk, Laura: *"Cancer. Would it kill you to smile at your coworkers?"*

Of course, there were complaints about the late-November horoscopes. (Thankfully, they were all routed to the "Inside Living" page editor . . . me.) In my defense, some people actually preferred the new horoscopes. Not Virgos, of course, since they were treated to day after day of stunning disappointment—*"One star: you should try to be less vindictive and disloyal . . . One star: hope your new boyfriend doesn't mind your bad breath . . . One star: you're not even good at sex."*

I'm the first to admit that I went a little far on November 24, the day I read in the crossword puzzle that the clue to 9-Across was a Jamaican spice, saw that the answer was *Jerk*, and changed the clue to *Mark Aikins, e.g.* Yes, it was petty, but I was being forced to wage a war without getting within eight hundred feet of my enemy.

Yet, despite my constant barrage of single-star Virgo days and crossword puzzle salvos, I got no response from either of them. Tanya knew this was my page. She had to know I was behind her run of bad horoscopes. But I heard nothing. Some days I thought she was taunting me by not responding; other days I imagined she was so deeply mired in one-star hassles (traffic snarls and Internet outages) that she was incapable of responding.

Another possibility arose on the last day of November. I had just called in another phony customer complaint to Il Pattio ("The chicken breast was woefully undercooked; it had all the symptoms of salmonella.") and driven back to the house I now shared with my dad. That's when I found him on the kitchen floor, slumped in a corner, his artificial leg at an odd angle, fake foot still flat on the floor.

He was in what doctors called a diabetic coma—an obvious result of his nonstop drinking. "You need to take better care of him," the ER nurse said. But it wasn't until I filled out the insurance paperwork that I understood exactly how I'd failed my dad. I copied his date of birth from his driver's license: August 28, 1947. I knew his birthday, naturally, but it hadn't occurred to me until that moment.

My father was a Virgo.

IN THEIR glee to portray me as a bad employee, the suits failed to mention that on the very day my dad was fighting for his life in a hospital bed, I still reported to work. Of course, it was also that day, November 30, that my section editor responded to a complaint from the features syndicate, investigated, and called me into her office. ·

In the frenzy of meetings and recriminations that followed, I somehow got one last altered horoscope into the paper. Again, I don't mean to portray myself as some kind of primitive, moon-worshipping kook, but the next day, Virgos across Portland read a heartfelt plea: *Five stars: you'll get better. I'm sorry.*

•   •   •

DAD PULLED out of his hypoglycemic coma and returned home to live dryly, me at his side. I have purged his little house of alcohol. Dad drinks a lot of tomato juice now. Since I'm not working, we play game after game of cribbage, so much that I have begun to dream of myself as one of those pegs, making my way up and down the little board. I recently shared this dream with my court-ordered therapist. She wondered aloud if the dream had to do with my father's peg leg. So I told Dad about my dream and he said that he sometimes dreams his missing leg is living in a trailer in Livingston, Montana. I'm thinking of asking him to come to counseling with me.

And Tanya? Even after the *Oregonian* ran its "Public Apology to Our Readers," full of righteous puffery about how I "acted maliciously and recklessly," how I "broke the sacred trust between a newspaper and its readers," I hoped Tanya would at least glean the depth of my feelings for her. But I never heard a word. My probation officer and therapist have insisted, rightly I suppose, that I leave Tanya alone, but this afternoon I went to the store to get more tomato juice for Dad and I found myself down the block from her building again.

This time, however, it was different. I know it sounds crazy, but I'd begun to worry that my little prank had some-how caused her to get sick. And I take it as a positive sign that I didn't want that for her. I really didn't. I sat in my car down the street and gazed up to our third-floor corner window, just hoping to get a glimpse of her. It's winter now and the early night sky was bruised and dusky. Our old condo was dark. It crossed my mind that maybe she had moved, and I have to say, I was okay with that. I had just reached down to start my car when I saw them walking up the sidewalk, a block from the condo. Tanya looked not only healthy, but beautiful. Happy. The big, dumb, sensitive, cheating chef was holding her hand. And I was happy for her. I really was. She laughed, and above them a streetlight winked at me and slowly came on.

There was a line in the newspaper's apology that stunned me, describing what I'd done as "a kind of public stalking." I shook when I read that. I suppose it's what Tanya thinks of me too. Maybe everyone. That I'm crazy. And maybe I am.

But if you really want my side of the story, here it is: Who isn't crazy sometimes? Who hasn't driven around a block hoping a certain person will come out; who hasn't haunted a certain coffee shop, or stared obsessively at an old picture; who hasn't toiled over every word in a letter, taken four hours to write a two-sentence e-mail, watched the phone praying that it will ring; who doesn't lay awake at night sick with the image of her sleeping with someone else?

I mean, Christ, seriously, *what love isn't crazy?*

And maybe it was further delusion, but as I sat in the car down the block from our old building, I was no longer wishing she'd take me back. Honestly, all I hoped was that Tanya at least thought of me when she read our page.

I really do think I'm better.

And so when I started the car to go home, and they crossed the street toward Tanya's condo, I was as surprised as anyone to feel the ache come back, an ache as deep and raw as the one I felt that night in late October when I first saw the lamp go out.

I told the other officer, the one at the scene, that I didn't re-member what happened next, though that's not entirely true.

I remember the throaty sound of the racing engine. I remember the feel of cutting across traffic, of grazing something—a car, they told me later—and I remember popping up on the sidewalk and scraping the light pole and I remember bearing down on the jutting corner of the building and I remember a slight hesitation as they started to turn. But what I remember most is a spreading sense of relief that it would all be over soon, that I would never again have to see the light come on in that cold apartment.

HELPLESS LITTLE THINGS

I FUCKING HATE PORTLAND.

It's so earnest and smug. There was a Portland guy here in Shelton on a meth pop and even he had it—that too-sweet-to-believe thing. Like a lot of chalkers, the guy's teeth were rotted, so he couldn't say his *R*s and I used to fuck with him about it.

So you're from Poland?

Po'tland, the dude would say calmly.

So you prefer being called Polish or Polack?

No, I'm f'om Po'tland.

Fuck off, Polack.

Then one day on yard, someone racked the poor helpless guy for standing too close and knocked out two of those black, hollow uppers. It was weird—afterward he could say his *R*s again, but he had a low humming whistle whenever he spoke. So we called him Kenny G. He actually believed this was an improvement.

I suppose I've hated Portland since I took a pop there. It was a shame, too, because it was the perfect Portland scam. A guy in my building was a volunteer recruiter for Greenpeace, and one day when he left his car unlocked I stole his pamphlets and sign-up logs. I couldn't use that shit in Seattle so I drove to Union Station in Portland, picked out two lost kids who looked like they could be college students, and put them out downtown. There was a girl, a little redhead named Julie, and a loaf named Kevin. I put gay Kevin on Burnside a block from Powell's and sweet Julie on Broadway, on the corner in front of Nordstrom.

Kevin was okay—friendly, made good eye contact—but Julie was the find: nineteen, short curly red hair, and what looked like a decent body under her hippy dress. She'd been kicked out of her house for accusing her stepdad of feeling her up, and though I'd heard that story a hundred times, it was harsh coming from her, because, like a lot of good-looking girls, she seemed convinced it was her fault.

I figured the bookstore would be the better place, but it wasn't even close to Julie's haul at Nordstrom—no one more eager to help the environment than a guilty white liberal dropping sixty on a tie. But then I switched them and Julie kicked ass at the bookstore, too, so it was all her.

It was almost too easy: the kids stopped shoppers, flashed a Greenpeace brochure, and asked them to join. Thankfully, most people don't want to join, or claim they're already members, but they're more than happy to give a one-time donation, especially when the kids say they're trying to raise four grand to go on the big Greenpeace ship that disrupts whaling. I'd printed up some tax-deduction receipts off the IRS website, and it was amazing how this convinced people we were legitimate. This was the cash side of the business: fives, tens, twenties, a few fifties. On the first day alone, Kevin got almost four hundred and Julie took in six-and-a-half. I chopped half, five-twenty-five for running the thing, and then sold Kevin some weed for the rest of his take. I tried to sell Julie some, too, but she shook her head. *I need money more than I need weed, Danny.*

Of course, some shoppers got nervous or suspicious and didn't want to give cash, or claimed they had none. This was fine. Like I told the kids: *Make them* want *to give you the thing you're taking.* So the kids would reluctantly mention credit cards and checks, but say that Greenpeace discouraged it. And they said they'd need to see some ID. Nothing kills suspicion like suspicion.

That was the real haul: credit card numbers and checks. I gave the kids twenty bucks for every card number but I got four hundred dollars each from a guy in Mexico; in two weeks I had given him seventeen. Give me your number and I can have four grand run on your card in Mexico before you've put your wallet away.

Checks were even easier. In Seattle I had a dude did nothing but print up phony checks. He had an ID template that made temporary driver's licenses and soon we were running phony checks all over the state.

This was all a nice diversion from my real business, running bud down from BC. My territory was Washington and Oregon, from Bellingham all the way down I-5. I had seven stops: Seattle, Tacoma, Olympia, Portland, Eugene, Salem, and Ashland. Two trips a week, up and back, meant two nights a week in the midpoint, Portland. People have a certain picture in their mind of a bud smuggler—white-boy dreds, Marley T-shirt—but I'd be a moron to dress like that for fifteen hundred miles a week with six kilos in the trunk. So I wore a suit and kept my hair short, hard-parted on the side, like a fifties superhero. But the key was my car: I had to be the youngest man in America in a loaded gray 2006 Buick Lucerne. Cop could pull me over blazing a spliff, coke spoon up my nose, syringe hanging from my tied-off arm, dead hooker in the passenger seat and still just tell me to ease off the gas and have a nice day.

No game works forever, of course, and I knew the Greenpeace thing could bust a hundred ways: kids steal from me, marks get suspicious, credit card companies get a whiff, real Greenpeacies get pissed. I put the half-life at three months. This was early November, so I figured I'd run the game at least through Christmas—when the banks and credit card companies are too busy to notice the extra draws—make a little side money and move on. In the meantime, I was careful. On my return run through Portland I always collected the Greenpeace material so the kids couldn't freelance. I moved Julie and Kevin around and worked hard to stay away from real fundraisers.

And once each, I had the kids strip in front of me, to make sure they weren't holding any money back. This is drastic shit, but you do it right, it only has to happen once. It makes a real impact, kid standing in front of you freezing his ass off while you go through his clothes. You make him stand a long time too, while you ignore him. Then, at the end—so he knows how far you'll go—you have him spread his ass cheeks, like a jail search. This is always necessary with drug dealers, but even if it weren't I'd do it anyway, to remind these kids that they're nothing. Meat.

I'll be the first to admit I was looking forward to this with little Julie. It wasn't like she had a stripper's body; she was small. I wasn't into the waif thing. But there was something about the way she moved, like poured syrup, and I couldn't help being curious about what lay underneath all those clothes.

Like my car, I chose my hotel rooms carefully. No sketchy motels for me. In Portland, I took a room at the Heathman downtown. I liked the porters in their Beefeater costumes, and I liked sitting on the mezzanine by the fire, drinking Chivas, and making eyes with the businesswomen. That's what did it for me, women in suits, not little homeless girls. My first night at the Heathman I hit a blonde prescription drug rep— impeccable makeup, Pilates-hard ass. *I'm in the same business*, I said. I wouldn't be surprised if they had to re-drywall my room after we were done banging around in it.

I was a month into the Portland gig when I called Julie up to my room. I sat on the big fluffy bed and told her to disrobe. Right away these big tears rolled over her cheeks.

No, it's not that, I said. I just need to make sure you're not stealing. I'd strip-searched Kevin a week earlier and he'd thrown a fit. *Danny, how could you think I'd ever steal from you?* But Julie just nodded, turned away from me, looked out the window, and started unbuttoning. I couldn't believe how many layers she was wearing—wool scarves and flannel and army surplus. And then there was just . . . her. Pale little body. Freckled shoulders. She was shaking. She turned away. I could see every little bump in her spine. It was her back that got to me, in fact, tapering down to this tiny waist, which I could've put my two hands completely around.

Then she started crying, in these jerking little hiccups.

I don't think I've ever felt worse in my life. She was so *small*. Not a tattoo or a ring anywhere. I turned away as I went through her clothes. They were warm. I've never felt so horny and so shitty at the same time.

Hell, I knew she wasn't stealing from me; she was outdrawing Kevin two-to-one.

It's okay, honey, I said. *You can get dressed now.*

I didn't touch her, and still the strip search changed things between Julie and me. She stopped meeting my eyes. Even her take started to go down. I'd watch from coffee shops and it was like she was shrinking. Where before she stepped up to shoppers, now she huddled against the wall, waiting for them to make eye contact. Soon Kevin was outdrawing her. This happens to dealers, too: they lose nerve and start shrinking, until, finally, they're done.

One day in mid-December, toward the end of the deal, I bought Julie and Kevin each a slice of pizza at the place across from Powell's. I explained that we were going to have to quit after Christmas, but that I'd use them for other things if they wanted work. Of course, I wasn't really going to use them again; but you always want them to think that you might have more money for them so they stay loyal.

I'm up for anything, Kevin said quickly.

Julie said nothing.

How about you? I asked her.

You don't want her, Kevin said.

Kevin and Julie had some sort of secret. She shoved him like she was trying to shush a seven-year-old.

What's goin' on, I asked.

Julie gave her money to Greenpeace, Kevin said, and then he broke into laughter.

She just stared at the ground as Kevin told the story. She'd gone to that shaggy Saturday market in Old Town and there was a Greenpeace booth under the Burnside Bridge. She'd stood there reading the material and looking at these kids behind the booth—so earnest, such believers. And then she just . . . snapped—took all the money she'd saved from our gig, almost twelve hundred bucks, and donated it.

Christ, Julie, I said.

But that's not all, Kevin said. *Then she tried to get me to donate my money, too.* This was what really broke him up.

As Kevin told the story, Julie's eyes got teary again. *It made me feel better*, she said quietly. Then to Kevin: *I thought you might want to feel better, too.*

I feel fine, he said, as he bit into his pizza.

Julie, I asked gently. *You think what we're doing is wrong?*

She gave a tiny nod.

That's because it is wrong, Julie, I said. *I'm the West Coast distributor of wrong.* I leaned forward. *Now I could tell you that we're no different than any other business or some shit like that. I could tell you a million lies, Julie, but just ask yourself this: do you think for one second those kids at the market can save a fucking whale?*

She looked up. *They can try.*

Come on. You know this is a hard goddamn world. You know what the world does to helpless things, don't you, Julie?

Yes, she whispered.

That's right, I said. *You know. Those whales are fucked. So fuck the businessmen and fuck Nordstrom and fuck your creepy stepdad and your blind mother. And if you wanna go home to your mom and her husband and save the whales, then fuck you too, Julie.*

Now, I've given this speech—or some variation of it— fifty times. But I've never had happen what happened with little Julie. She jerked a little when I mentioned her stepdad and mom and then she stood up. *You're right, Danny*, she said. *Thanks.*

And just like that she walked away.

I know a girl we can get, Kevin said.

I just sat there, watching her walk away, thinking about the sliver of girl who lived under those clothes—that back, that waist—and wishing I'd said something else. So that was it. We were done. I told Kevin I'd see him in two days, when I came back through Portland, but I didn't figure to see either of them ever again.

That week I picked up my regular load in Bellingham and started south. I made my drop in Seattle and collected the money, made my drop in Olympia and collected the money, and I drove south on I-5 toward Portland. I hadn't been able to stop thinking about little Julie. And I didn't really plan to do it, but I got off the freeway and drove to Union Station, where I'd met them.

Kevin was there. I tried to ask casually about Julie.

She got the shit kicked out of her, he said.

Who did it, I asked.

He shrugged. He said she sometimes hung out in this boho coffee shop, and sure enough that's where I found her, in this foul, patchouli-smelling shithole, reading a book, wrapped up in those layers of hippy clothes. When I got closer I could see a yellowing bruise below her eye. Her bottom lip was fat.

She flinched when she saw me.

Who did this? I asked.

She looked confused. *No one.*

And that's when I knew. *You went home, didn't you? After I told you to. Did your stepdad do this, Julie?*

Those tears again. She stared down at her lap and sobbed.

I sat in the booth next to her and put my arm around her. Carefully, like she was made of glass. *It's okay*, I said.

I took her to the Heathman. The valet tipped his silly

British hat to her, and she smiled. I took her upstairs so she could shower and clean up. I wanted to be in that room, but I also didn't want to be in that room. I went to Nordstrom and bought her some clothes. She was wearing the white terrycloth hotel robe when I got back, staring out the window. I left the clothes on the bed and told her I'd be downstairs in the mezzanine.

The clothes were too big—a pair of pants, a sweater, and a heavy coat—but she didn't seem to mind. We ate on the mezzanine, in front of the fire. She glanced up at me once over the tall menu. She said she was vegan. Of course. When she ordered *sun-dried tomato pasto ravioli* I wanted to kick the waiter's ass when he corrected her: *pesto*.

She ate like it was her last meal. I was careful not to talk about anything. When we were done, I had the valet get the car. We climbed in. It was eight-thirty.

I told her what I wanted to do.

No, she said. *Please don't. It will make it worse.*

Listen, I said. *I promise you . . . whatever happens, this will not make it worse.* I wanted to grab her hand, but I didn't. *This is a hard world, Julie. That's all.*

They lived in Beaverton. We turned in front of this little strip mall; she smiled and pointed at the Coffee People where she used to work. She stared out the window and shrank inside her new coat as we got close.

That one, she said in a whisper. I parked. It was a big white house leaning out on four big porch pillars. Everything about the house pissed me off—the black shutters, the Christmas lights. But what really got me was the black BMW in the driveway. Here I was driving a Buick Lucerne and this molester rolled in a BMW?

Please, she said. *I changed my mind. Don't. Let's just go.*

I grabbed her little shoulders. *Listen. I'm gonna talk to him. I'm not going to hurt him. Okay?*

Then she grabbed me and hugged me and even under the sweater and the new coat I could feel that tiny back. She was shaking. I turned the heat up, pushed her gently back into her seat, and climbed out.

I walked up to the house and rang the bell. There was a little reindeer next to the door. Honestly, I don't know what I was planning to do. All I know is that when he answered the door, something about him set me off.

He was probably fifty, with black hair parted on the side like mine. He was in good shape, but his face was flabby, like he'd recently lost a bunch of weight.

Can I help you? he asked.

It was as if my hands belonged to someone else. I pushed him backward into the house. *I don't know*, I said. Can *you fuckin' help me?*

He fell and scrambled backward.

I kicked him, a dull sound, like someone clapping with gloves on. *Yeah, you* can *help me, you fuckin' child molester.* And that's when I realized I was going to kill him. I've done a lot of shit, but I'd never killed a guy before.

He crab crawled toward the steps. *Deb!*

And a woman called from upstairs, *Carl?*

Stay in your room, Deb! I yelled up the stairs. And I kicked him again, harder, in the ribs. It took the wind out of him, and he collapsed against the stairs. God, I wanted to kill him. But I thought of Julie, and I bent down and took him by the hair and spoke calmly into his ear. *You ever touch her again, and I'll kill you so slowly you won't even realize you're dead. Do you understand me,* stepdad?

Yes, he said. *Please. . .*

And even though I wanted to keep stomping him, I stood and started for the door. Restraint: that's what keeps a guy in business. On the foyer wall were pictures of Deb and Carl and two little kids. The assholes didn't even have a picture of her.

I think that's when I knew. I stepped out onto the front porch. The Lucerne was gone. I stood there a minute doing the math. I patted my suit coat. My wallet was gone. The hug. Sure. I glanced back at the house, wondering how she'd chosen it. Did her actual parents live around here, or was it just random? In a hatch in the trunk of my car was sixty grand from my Seattle, Olympia, and Portland drops. I hadn't made the Salem, Eugene, and Ashland drops so there was another thirty or forty thousand in weed behind that hatch. I stood on that porch, thrilled by the audacity of it all, a moron's smile on my face.

Every pop is bad luck. Who'd have thought, for instance, that as nice as that neighborhood was, a cop would live nearby? But a property crimes detective was kitty corner, and apparently Deb had called him from upstairs. So while I stood grinning on the porch, the fat son-of-a-bitch came huffing across the street, yelling and drawing down on me. I had no choice but to drop and put my arms out.

I was still smiling as he cuffed me, and still when they hauled me in front of a judge the next morning and arraigned me on assault charges.

I have a great lawyer, a guy who does more contracts work than defense stuff, but even he said I was screwed. I had apparently really scared poor Carl, who, coincidentally, was the stepfather to those kids in the picture. I bonded out and eventually pled to a misdemeanor assault with a big fine and restitution but no jail time. I had to send Carl a letter of apology. I sort of told the truth—that I had the wrong house and I was sorry. Of course, I had to replace the Lucerne, and make good on the money and dope that Julie stole, but in a way I was lucky. What if I'd killed poor Carl? For nothing.

I didn't like spending the night in Portland after that, but I did stop a few times to ask around about her. It was as if she'd never existed. I found the puff Kevin working at a Quiznos, but I was convinced she'd played him, too. He didn't even know her last name. I asked about the day she got beat up. *Did she tell you to tell me about it?*

No, he said. *She said it was nothing and I shouldn't worry about it.*

It was all so subtle. Amazing . . . all of it. I'd made my share of mistakes—selling weed to Kevin so that she figured out what I was doing in Portland; falling for that crying shit; leaving the car running because she was cold.

But it wasn't me. It was all her. It was all so subtle; she'd just let the whole thing come to her. *Make them want to give you the thing you want to take.*

Everything felt . . . fragile after that. Something like that happens and it shakes you. And once you realize how creaky and frail everything is, you start to imagine yourself making mistakes. And then, I suppose, it's just a matter of time.

I had always figured the roll would come from below, but when I finally got ratted, it was by the guy on top, the guy I bought my dope from. He wore a wire for a month while they had me under surveillance. They even had GPS on my car to get my contacts. Four months to the day after Julie scammed me, they arrested me with four pounds of bud in the back of the new Lucerne. I pled to six years.

Four days before that arrest, I spent one last night in Portland. I hadn't planned to do it, but I was tired. And maybe nostalgic. I got a room at the Heathman, sat on the mezzanine, and had the sun-dried tomato pesto ravioli. Next morning, I went down to Old Town for the Saturday Market. The place was full of shitty artists, tie-dyed deadheads, and pottery assholes selling henna tattoos and alpaca scarves.

There was no Greenpeace booth.

I was about to leave when I saw her, skinny little redhead boho chick walking away from me, wearing the coat I'd bought Julie that day. I ran after her. *Hey!*

I didn't know what I was going to do. I just wanted to talk to her.

But when the girl turned, it wasn't Julie. Just a redhead in a coat. *I'm sorry*, I said. *My mistake.* She said, *It's okay.*

It is a hard goddamn world. But for a second or two, this redhead girl and I stood still in it as people moved all around us, like two stones in a river.

PLEASE

TOMMY GOT HIS KID SATURDAY, first time in three weeks. —What the hell, Carla?

—My folks made us stay a extra day I swear.

Carla's boyfriend Jeff was twitching, yellow-eyed, had a big red abscess on his arm. He worked his jaw, didn't even look up from the TV.

Tommy sent the kid to the truck. On the front porch he leaned in to Carla. —Your boyfriend's chalked up.

Carla flinched. —No he ain't.

Tommy left her, walked to the truck. —Hey Dad, the kid said.

—Mom stay with you at Grand-mom's last week?

—No. Just me and Grand-mom.

—She take you for that pizza you like?

—Yeah. With them balls you jump in. Grand-mom couldn't have no pizza 'cause a the tube in her stomach.

Tommy fired the truck. He was relieved it rolled over. —Know where your mom went to?

The kid shook his head. —I found a dollar in them balls.

They went to the mini-golf. Tommy parked on a hill in case he had to coast-start. The kid didn't hold the putter right. Tommy thought he did good anyway.

—Jeff ever watch you hisself?

—Sometimes.

—He take you anyplace?

The kid looked up. —I ain't supposed to say.

—You ain't supposed to keep secrets neither.

—We go to stores.

—Grocery stores?

—Yeah.

—How many?

—I don't know. Lots.

—Other people go?

—Yeah.

—They buy cold medicine and stuff?

—Uh-huh.

—Then what, you all meet back at the car?

—It's a van.

They had nachos for dinner. And Pepsis.

Back at Carla's, Tommy had the kid wait in the truck. Took the steps two at a time and didn't knock. Had Jeff against the wall fast. —Stay away from him.

Jeff didn't say a thing. Carla neither.

Tommy wanted something hard to hit but Jeff was soft. Empty clothes. So he turned to Carla. —Leave the kid with me if you're gonna do that shit.

And then he said —Please.

That was the thing. Didn't even know why he said it. But after the boy went inside Tommy sat out front in his truck, shaking with something. He just kept thinking that word, *please*, Carla standing dumb at the window, chewing a nail and watching him.

DON'T EAT CAT

1

AT NIGHT I DEADBOLT doors and hard-bar windows, and it's not bad living in the city. I stay home a lot. Turn off outdoor lights, bring in garbage cans: simple, commonsense stuff. Obviously, I don't have pets. I leave my car unlocked so they won't break the windows looking for food and trinkets. Play low music all night to drown out the yowling. But nights aren't bad. Daytime is when I get fed up with zombies.

I know. I shouldn't call them that.

I'm not one of those reactionaries who believes they should be locked up, or sterilized, or confined to Z-Towns. I think there are perfectly good jobs for people with *hypo-endocrinal-thyro-encephalitis*: day labor, night janitors. But hiring zombies for food service? I just think that's wrong.

That particular day, I'd had another doctor's appointment, and had gotten the unhappy results from a battery of invasive tests. I was already late for a sim-skype in Jakarta when I popped into the Starbucks-Financial near my office. I got to the front of the line and who should greet me behind the counter but some guy in his early twenties with all the

symptoms: translucent skin, rotting teeth, skim-milk eyes—
the whole deal. Full zombie. (I know: We shouldn't call them
that.)

His voice was ice in a blender. "I help you."

"Grande. Soy. Cran. Latte," I said as clearly and as patiently as possible.

He said back to me in that curdled grunt: "Gramma sing
con verde?"

I stared at him. "Grande . . . Soy . . . Cran . . . Latte."

"Gramma say come hurry?" His dull eyes blinked, and he
must've heard the impatience in my voice—"No!"—because
he started humming the way they do when they get agitated.
"Gran-maw!" he yelled, and the manager, standing at the
drive-thru banking/coffee window behind him, turned and
gave me a look like, *Dude* . . . and I looked back at the manager (you're blaming *me* for this?). The other people in the
Starbucks-Financial all took a step back.

Look, I understand the economics. I work in multinational
food/finance. I know there has been some difficulty in staff-
ing service jobs in the States since the borders were closed.
More than that, I get the *humanity* of hiring them. Hey, my ex-
girlfriend started shooting Replexen *after* researchers made
the connection between hypo-ETE and the popular club
drug. Marci actually *chose* that life. So, yes, I know how their
brains work; I know abstraction and contextual language
give them problems; I know they're prone to agitation; but I
also know that, as long as they're not drunk or riled up, zombies can be as peaceful as anyone. And yes, I know we're not
supposed to call them zombies.

But come on? *Gramma sing con verde?* What does that even
mean?

That day, the Starbucks-Financial manager came over and put a hand on the zombie's shoulder. "You're doing fine, Brando," the manager said. He was in his fifties, in a head-set, tie, and short sleeves, one of those sorry men who try to overcome a lack of education and breeding by working up from food service into retail finance. The manager smiled at me and then pointed to "latte" on Brando's touch-screen sim, and they debited the sixty bucks from my iVice while I walked over to the other line. And over at the drink counter who should be making my actual coffee but another zombie, a girl who couldn't have been more than eighteen, standing there dead-gaze-steaming my soy milk.

Two zombies. At morning rush hour. In a Starbucks-Financial. In the multi-nat/finance district of downtown Se-attle. Really?

The manager was watching the girl zombie steam my milk when Brando screwed up the next order, too, turning a simple double cappuccino into "Dapple *cat* beano—", a hungry hitch on that word *cat*, and you could feel the other businesspeople in the Starbucks-Financial tense, and even the short-sleeved manager knew this could be trouble, no doubt thinking back to their training (apparently, they put four or five of them in a room with an actual cat and repeat-edly stress *DON'T EAT CAT*, which has to be tough when every fiber of the zombie's being is telling him to *EAT CAT*); and in the meantime, poor Brando was humming, just about full tilt. At that point, of course, the manager should have called the Starbucks-Financial security guards to come over from the banking side or called whatever priva-police firm had that contract, but instead he put a hand up to the dozen or so of us in the store and he walked calmly over to the kid

and said, "Brando, why don't you go into the break room
and relax for a few minutes." But Brando's red-veined eyes
were darting around the room and he started making those
deeper guttural noises, and look, I was not without sympathy
for the manager, or for Brando, or for the twitchy zombie
girl running the steamer, who looked over at her fish-skinned
counterpart, both of them now thinking *ca-a-a-at*, salivating
like someone had yelled chocolate in a kindergarten, the girl
zombie humming too now, the soy milk for my latte climbing
to two hundred degrees—"Miss," I said—and still my soy
was hissing and burbling, half to China Syndrome, the boiling riling everyone up, the manager calmly saying "Brando,
Brando, Brando," and I suppose I was still freaked by the
bad news from my doctor's appointment, because I admit
it, I raised my voice: "Miss, you're *burning* it," and when she
didn't even acknowledge me, just kept humming and watching Brando, I clapped my hands and yelled, "Stop it!" And
that's when the manager shot me a look that said *You're not
helping!* And hell, I knew I wasn't helping, but who doesn't get
frustrated, I mean, I wouldn't want that manager's life and I
certainly wouldn't want to be some twenty-one-year-old with
full-on Hypo-ETE but we all have our crosses to bear, right?
I just wanted a stupid cup of coffee. And I'd have stormed out
right then, but my iVice had already been debited and I suppose there was something else too, something personal—I'm
willing to acknowledge that—I mean how would *you* feel if
your girlfriend got so depressed that she actually *chose* to start
taking Replexen, knowing it could make her a slow-witted,
oversexed night-crawler, how would you feel if the woman
you loved actually CHOSE zombie life (I know, we're not
supposed to . . .) over the apparently unbearable pain of a

normal life with you? So *fuck-me sue-me yes yes yes* I was short-tempered! You bet your ass I was short-tempered, and I yelled at that poor pale girl, "Hey Zombie! You're scalding my fucking latte!"

I know.

We're not supposed to call them zombies.

What was I supposed to say, "Excuse me, *unfortunate sufferer of hypo-endocrinal-thyro-encephalitis*, please stop burning my coffee"?

I suppose it was inevitable what happened next. As it unfolded I felt awful. I still feel awful—but in my defense, I *was* the only customer who didn't turn and run right then, as Brando flashed his teeth and pit-bulled the manager, leaped right into the poor guy's chest, both of them tumbling to the ground. In fact, I actually tried to distract him, clapping my hands and yelling as he worked over the poor screaming manager. And to be fair, Brando didn't get far. *He bit but he didn't chew . . .* is I guess how you'd say it. He really wasn't trying to *eat* the manager. He was just scared and agitated. Probably not a distinction the manager was making at that time, with Brando yowling, biting and scratching, sinewy veins popping beneath translucent skin, the manager lying on his back, covering his face, weeping, *"Oh God,"* as Brando snarled and struck and the girl zombie yowled in sympathy, still standing there, steaming my soy milk, which was like magma now, gurgling over the side of the pitcher. And if I give myself credit for anything, it's thinking quickly on my feet. I grabbed the scalding pitcher out of her hand and threw the boiling milk on Brando, who reared his head like a bridled horse, snarled and spun on me as I turned and ran for the door, Brando now bounding over the counter and toward me like a hungry wolf, knocking over

displays of coffee cups and food-mortgage brochures as he
ran straight into the arms of two Starbucks-Financial security
guys, who quickly Tasered the poor guy to the ground and,
eventually, into submission.

I stood on the sidewalk with the gathered crowd as the
security guys loaded the hog-tied, muzzled Brando into the
back of a Halliburton priva-police car, the poor kid still
making that awful yowling noise, which shivered up my neck.

"What happened?" a young man asked.

"Zombie attack," a woman said.

I muttered, "You're not supposed to call them that."

It was the first documented attack in months and the
sim-tweets went crazy, as they always do when the subject
is Hypo-ETE. The tweet was up for hours, twice as long as
any election news; only the Florida evacuation tweet was
up longer that week. Most of the noise came from Apocalyptics ranting about Revelations, law-and-order types calling for another crackdown on Replexen, and on the other
side Hypo-ETE activists calling for mercy, for understanding, and for more government funding for programs aimed at
those kids *born into* Replexen addiction, family support groups
accusing the "irate customer" of being an agitator (thankfully, I wasn't named). Starbucks-Financial stock dropped
a couple of points after that (I managed to short the whole
coffee finance sector for my Indonesian clients), and the company announced it would "revisit its Hypo-ETE retraining
program." But, honestly, it just seemed like the whole thing
would fade. The manager would get a good payout, I'd get a
free latte, the zombies would get retrained ("Brando. Do not
eat cat."), and the world would go on. Or so I thought.

2

EVERYONE HAS an opinion about when it all went to hell: this war, that epidemic, the ten billion people threshold, the twelve, this environmental disaster, the repeated economic collapses, suicide pacts, anti-procreation laws, nuclear accidents, terrorist dirty bombs, polar thaws, rolling famines— blah blah blah, it's getting to where you can't watch the sim-tweets without someone saying *this* is the end of the world or *that*—genetic piracy, food factory contaminations, the Wasatch uprising, Saudi death squads, the Arizona border war. Animal extinctions. Ozone tumors. And, of course, the so-called zombie drug.

But here's what I've come to believe. That maybe it's no different now than it ever was. Maybe it's ALWAYS the end of the world. Maybe you're alive for a while, and then you realize you're going to die, and that's such an insane thing to comprehend, you look around for answers and the only answer is that the world *must die* with you.

Sure, the world seems crazy *now*. But wouldn't it seem just as crazy if you were alive when they sacrificed peasants, when people were born into slavery, when they killed first-born sons, crucified priests, fed people to lions, burned them on stakes, when they intentionally gave people smallpox or syphilis, when they gassed them, burned them, dropped atomic bombs on them, when entire races tried to wipe other races off the planet?

Yes, we've ruined the planet and melted the ice caps and depleted the ozone, and we're always finding new ways to kill one another. Yeah, we're getting cancer at an alarming rate and suicides are at an all-time high, and, sure, we've got people so depressed they take a drug that could turn them into pasty-skinned animals who go around all night dancing and having sex and eating stray cats and small dogs and squirrels and mice and very, *very rarely*—the statistics say you're more likely to be killed by lightning—a person.

But *this* is the Apocalypse? Fuck you! It's always the Apocalypse. The world hasn't gone to shit. The world *is* shit.

All I'd asked was that it be better managed.

But four days after the Starbucks-Financial incident, Apocalyptics began protesting Starbucks-Financial headquarters and the company announced the complete suspension of its zombie retraining program, which got the Hypo-ETE activists and support groups going again about the 60 percent zombie unemployment rate. Then, worst of all, some vigilantes came to Seattle from the country and killed a nineteen-year-old zombie girl with an antique hunting rifle, shot her outside a club and left her body outside a Starbucks-Financial.

All because I'd wanted better service.

The dead zombie girl was all over the news-tweets. I couldn't stop staring at her photo. Her ashen-white skin glistened in the blue light. Of course it wasn't Marci; it looked nothing like her, but I couldn't stop thinking about my old girlfriend. I sat that night in our apartment on Queen Anne Hill, staring at the results from my full body scan, the doors and windows double-locked, low music playing, and I wondered if things might have been different.

3

MARCI HAD a cousin who went zombie a few years back, before it was called that. It was the usual thing: Stephanie came from a poor family, got low scores on her sixth-grade E-RADs—we're talking food-service low, back-labor low.

Imagine being a twelve-year-old girl and being told that all you can ever aspire to is greeter at a Walmart-Schwab. Stephanie had childhood diabetes, and since her parents' application for gene therapy had been rejected, her own chances of getting a childbirth license were nil. So she started snorting Replexen. This was right after kids in clubs discovered that grinding up the weight-loss/metabolism-boosting pill could give them an ungodly buzz, slow time, allow them to dance and screw all night, and although it was already connected to the symptoms of Hypo-ETE—milky eyes, pale skin, increased hunger, slow-witted aggressiveness—it didn't stop them. For some, that only seemed to make the high better.

One day, Marci and I were watching sim-tweets of the Northeast Portland Riots—during the debate over anti-harassment laws and the whole Don't-Call-Them-Zombies campaign.

"Poor Stephanie," I said.

"I don't know," Marci said. "Maybe she knew what she was doing."

Afterward, people at work would ask me, Did you suspect? Of course, after someone leaves, you find all sorts of clues, look back on conversations that suddenly have great significance, but honestly, that's the first thing I remember, Marci saying about her zombie cousin, *Maybe she knew what she was doing.*

Of course, I had known for some time that Marci wasn't happy. Our last couple of years had been tough on her, tough on both of us. Most of our friends had moved out of the city. Our apartment had lost most of its value. That fall, our procreation application had been red-flagged—Marci's gene scan had uncovered some recessive issue. I told her I didn't care if we had a kid. But it became part of the class stuff between us: I was from money, Marci wasn't; I'd aced my E-RADs and Gen-Tests; she'd been borderline in both. None of that had mattered when we'd started seeing each other. And it still didn't for me. But when the procreation board said she couldn't have a kid? I guess it was too much for her.

But did I know Marci was using Replexen? I don't think so. It's hard to separate what you suspect from what you know later. Certainly, she seemed *off* that spring, disoriented, nervous, wearing more makeup, eating more, yet somehow getting thinner. Then I got promoted at work, to the Asian desk, only days after Marci's job was eliminated. We're fine, I kept telling her, and I meant financially. But it must have seemed insane to her, the way I just kept saying we were fine. That March there was a story on the sim-tweets about a couple in the Magnolia neighborhood who had chosen to go zombie. I turned away from the screen to Marci and I just . . . asked. *Would you ever?*

I think she'd been waiting for me to bring it up. "Yes," she said quietly.

"Yes, what?" I asked.

Yes, she had used Replexen. A few times. Snorted it.

I asked, "Recently?" She slumped in her chair.

"Yes," she said.

"How recently?"

"I'm using it now," she whispered.

We were in the living room. I stood. And for some reason, the question that popped into my mind was this one: "Where did you get it?"

She glanced up at me and, in that moment, I suppose we were thinking the same thing—why, when Marci tells me she's taking the most dangerous club drug in the world, the first thing to pop into my mind would not be her health, but where she had gotten it.

A few months earlier, Marci and I had gone through an especially difficult time. Her company had just been bought up and the inevitable squeeze had begun. Marci had wanted to leave Seattle, to move closer to her family, but my company was thriving, so I said no. She said I was imperious and blind to reality; I said she was defeatist. We split up for a few weeks before we realized we'd made a mistake and got back to-gether. It was only after she came back that time that I began to suspect Marci had gone back to her previous boyfriend, Andrew. He was a club owner and a *nonbie*, one of the lucky fifteen percent who could use Replexen without any of the undesirable zombie side effects.

So I asked: "Did you get the drugs from Andrew?"

"No," she said, "I got them from a woman I used to work with."

"What woman?"

"You don't know her."

"Why would you do that, Marci?"

"Oh, Owen," she said, "this isn't about you. It's about me."

It was the cliché that got to me. ("Yeah, you're right, it's about you, Marci . . . *you're becoming a fucking zombie!*") I yanked her sleeve up and saw the red marks against her white skin, and Jesus, shooting it is twice as dangerous as snorting it. Once your skin starts to go you've already done permanent damage. She shrank away from me, cried, apolo-gized, promised to get treatment, and when we went to bed that night I honestly believed we could get through this, that we'd caught it in time. I spent the next day applying for loans from all the food-service-banks—Starbucks-Financial, Walmart-Schwab, KFC/B-of-A. I would have debited my apartment, my car, my organs for her treatment, but I came home from work that night and she was gone. No sim, no note, no nothing.

I simmed our friends and her parents, her old coworkers, but no one had heard from Marci. I even went to see her old boyfriend, Andrew, at his club in what was still called the U-District, even though the state university there had shut down years earlier. Andrew was bald and lean—a little taller than me, with a long neck and cavernous eyes, pock marks on his sunken cheeks. Nonbies always have that feral look, as if they just finished running a road race in their clothes, or they haven't slept in months. We had met once, in passing, but I would never have picked him out of a lineup, so many years had been put on his face. Andrew came from behind the bar, and I could smell the nonbie on him—like a soup of sweat, smoke, and old bacon. He stared at my suit and tie, at my wool coat.

"Slumming, Owen?"

I looked around the seedy club but said nothing.

He crossed his arms. "What do you want?"

I explained that Marci had started using Replexen and that she was missing. I watched his face to see if maybe he already knew what I was telling him. Andrew was wearing a black leather coat, too short on his arms. I saw one of his hands twitch. He stared at the door to his club. He let out a deep breath. "Was she snorting it?" he asked quietly.

"Needles," I said. His eyes closed, and I realized that he hadn't seen her after all. He asked about her skin. "Yes," I said, "milky."

"You didn't notice?" he asked. Then he looked down. "Sorry."

Even as a nonbie, Replexen use shortens your lifespan. They are hard years spent on that shit. I followed Andrew's weary eyes as he looked around his own club . . . painted windows and scarred wood on the tables and floors. Did he wonder, how did I get here? This wasn't a full zombie club, it catered more to nonbies and first-timers; no, it wasn't hell, but it was the waiting room.

"I haven't seen her," Andrew said, and he turned and went back behind the bar. I could've just simmed him my number, but I wrote it on a piece of paper and slid it across the bar. He looked up. He was chewing on one of those pocked cheeks, and it looked like he was trying to say something. I left before he could.

My guess was that Marci had disappeared into what was already starting to be called Z-Town. And if that was the case, of course, I was too late. Scattle was one of the worst cities for derelict zombies—old Fremont had been turned over to the hardcore clubs, brothels, and shooting galleries, to bars that supposedly released rodents during happy hour—places that made Andrew's shitty club seem like a Four Seasons.

For two years after that, I waited for Marci to come back. But it wasn't until my last doctor's appointment and the bad news I got, it wasn't until after Brando snapped and the death of that poor zombie girl, that I finally felt compelled to go to Z-Town and look for her, look for the only woman I have ever loved.

4

WENDY GASSON was the last of my neighbors to have a pet: Fidel. He was an indoor cat and she was careful about making sure he didn't get out, but one day, as Fidel sat there by the window watching birds, Wendy came in with the groceries and the cat bolted out the door, down the stairs, out the open front door, and into the street.

After the initial sim-tweets about Hypo-ETE, a new sector of the economy had appeared: private eyes who went into Z-Towns and looked for missing kids and spouses and took them to quack deprogrammers, or surgeons, a whole industry of people who promised—lied, really—that they could reverse the effects of long-term Replexen abuse. The sleaziest of these PIs would even take cat cases, usually for elderly people who just couldn't come to terms with the fact that Fluffy was *seriously* not coming back. Some of the private eyes just went to a pet store and got a tabby to match the pictures ("No, this is Fluffy; I'm sure of it."). Wendy told me she'd tried to hire one of these guys off the Craig-sim to find Fidel, but the guy only went after people. "Lady," he said, "your cat's gone."

I got the detective's name from Wendy, but I didn't contact him right away. I tried everything else I could think of first: simming Marci's friends and family, taking out Craig-sim ads. I even went back to Andrew's club in the U-District, but it was closed; a Dumpster Divas secondhand food store was now in its place. Nobody knew anything. I had no choice.

So I simmed the detective and made plans to meet him outside my doctor's office. I stepped out into the cool air, chest still burning from the radiation, when a tall gray guy in a long suede jacket stepped forward. "I'm Mick."

"Owen."

Mick was in his fifties, with a high forehead and severe blue eyes. I hadn't explained much in my tweet, but he didn't seem to want details. I followed him to an antique red hybrid and we climbed in. I asked where he found gas for this old car and he just smiled at me, like it was proof of his investigative powers.

It was a flat rate, he explained as we drove, five thousand up front.

I pulled out my iVice to debit him the five grand but he shook his head. "Cash," he said.

So we went to the nearest KFC-Bank of America, where I was pre-approved for the highest food debits. I lied on the application and said it was for dinner at a nice restaurant. Mick counted the five grand, folded the bills, tucked them in his waistband, and started driving. He pulled a small bottle of homemade hooch from beneath his car seat and handed it to me. I took a drink. Vodka.

I pulled out my iVice to show him the pictures of Marci, to tell him about her, but he held up his hand. "Save it till we get there." We drove quietly along Westlake.

"Get where?" I asked.

He chuckled at something. "Hey, what'd one zombie say to another?"

I stared at him. "What did you say?"

"What . . . did one zombie say to the other?"

"Is . . . that a joke?"

"*Dystopia?* What dystopia? Dis da only 'topia dere is."

I stared at him.

"You *do* know what a dystopia is, right?"

I said I did.

It was dusk as we approached the Fremont Bridge. Even before Fremont became Z-Town, the construction of the Aurora Tunnel had cut down on traffic crossing into Fremont. Now, it was six o'clock and there were maybe a dozen cars on the road. The bridge's cross-braces were covered with holo-boards warning about the dangers of Replexen abuse and reminding people it was illegal to transport "cats and other pets" into Fremont, and finally there was the big black and white sign: "WARNING: ENTERING HYPO-ETE CON- CENTRATION DISTRICT."

Mick held out the bottle again. "Couple looking for an affordable condo in Seattle calls a real estate agent," he said. "Agent says, I know a place, five rooms, city views. Bad news, it's in Zombietown. Good news? It's very pet-friendly."

I took a drink of his vodka, my hands shaking. The street- lights in Fremont were tinted blue—it's calming for them— and this gave everything a strange underwater glow, like an aquarium. There were few people on the streets—zombie or otherwise, the buildings nondescript, simple brick storefronts. We turned and started back toward the water. We passed Gasworks Park, and I imagined I saw figures moving in the shadows of the hulking works, flashing matches, bits of skin.

"How many zombies does it take to screw in a lightbulb?" Mick asked.

I closed my eyes. "Please," I whispered.

"UUUUNNNNGGG!" he said.

We turned again, and again, and back again, down a street with no lights, and I had the sense Mick was driving serpentine, to make me disoriented. Finally, we pulled up in front of a dark four-story building.

"This is it," Mick said.

I looked up at the building.

"You got those pictures of her?" he asked.

I held up my iVice.

Mick nodded and got out of the car. I followed him. We

stood in front of the building. I could hear yowling in the distance. I shivered as I stared at the dark building in front of us. "You haven't asked me a single question about Marci," I said. "What makes you think she'll even be here?"

Mick shrugged. "What's the worst part about having sex with a zombie?"

I put my hands up. "Please. No more jokes."

"Burying your cat afterward."

We climbed the stairs and pushed open a heavy door. We came into a dimly lit foyer, closed heavy doors on either end. A wall-mounted eye-cam pointed at us. Mick held up two thousand-dollar bills. He crinkled them. Then he opened his coat for the camera, I guess to show that he had no weapons. Then he elbowed me. I did the same, opened my coat.

After a moment, an electronic lock clicked and one of the doors opened and a muscular young zombie kid in baggy shorts, a sweatshirt, sunglasses, and flip-flops came through. At first I thought it was Brando, but, of course, it wasn't.

"Follow me," the zombie kid rasped.

I looked at Mick. "Aren't you coming?"

"What's the difference between a zombie and a bagel?" Mick asked. I just stared at him. *"UUUUNNNNGGG!"* he said again.

The zombie kid grunted a kind of laugh. "Good one, Mick."

Mick shrugged. "It kinda works with anything. *UUNNGG!"* Then he turned and went back outside. I watched him go, wondering if I should turn and follow him out. Instead, I hurried after the zombie kid. It was cold in the long hallway, clammy. Closed doors lined the walls; strange sounds came from the rooms. At the end of the hall, we came to a set of

doors that opened on a huge ballroom—a lounge of some
kind, heavy timbers and ornate molding, like an old social
club, an Elks Club maybe, smoky, filled with the movements
of people on overstuffed leather couches and chairs—and as
my eyes focused I could see a bar at the front and a couple
of zombies serving drinks. Everywhere else, white-skinned
women in scanty clothing lounged around, talking to men
like me.

It was a brothel.

"This is a mistake," I said to the kid.

The zombie kid turned and at first I thought he was staring at me, but he was looking at someone over my shoulder.
"Dina," said the zombie kid.

"You have pictures?" a woman asked from behind me.

I turned. The woman, Dina, was in her thirties, with
shimmery black hair, pale skin, her eyes that cloudy blue, but
somehow not entirely gone zombie yet, or just controlled in
some way. Like the kid who had led me back here. In fact,
there seemed to be a whole range here—not just zombies and
nonbies, but people who seemed to function under the effects
of the drug.

"You have pictures of your wife," Dina said again, her
voice just betraying the slightest hint of Hypo-ETE gravel.

"My girlfriend," I said.

She nodded, and smiled warmly at me.

I pulled out my iVice and fumbled with it. "I don't know
if she's . . . I mean . . . you don't think Marci is . . ." I glanced
around at the zombie prostitutes all around us. One of them
took a man by the hand and led him away.

Dina the zombie madam reached out and steadied my
hands. "It's okay. Relax."

Finally, I found a holo of Marci and me in our apartment—it was when she had short hair, but it was a great picture, her bemused chestnut eyes, long lashes, high cheekbones. The 3D holo appeared blurry rising from my iVice, but then I realized it was my eyes. I wiped the tears. Dina smiled. "She's so pretty."

I nodded and pulled the image back into my iVice.

"How long ago?"

"Two years. She left . . . two years ago."

Dina nodded again. She took my hand. I looked down at our hands, her white skin against my sun-scarred hand. She led me across the darkened room. I felt the breath go out of me. I was terrified I might see Marci here, terrified I might not.

We arrived at one of the couches, in the corner of the lounge, where a short-haired zombie girl was sitting, staring off blankly. On the table in front of her was a hypodermic syringe with a needle, and a bag of powder. "Is that—" I pointed at the drugs on the table.

Dina said, "It makes some men feel better to know what it's like."

"Oh no," I said, "I don't want that." Then I looked closely at the girl on the couch, her brown hair and eyes, her high cheekbones. I reached out, tilted her chin up. "You know that's not Marci," I said.

"Of course it is."

"No, it's not even close. This girl's ten years younger than Marci . . . at least three inches shorter."

"Marci," Dina said, and the zombie on the couch looked up at me.

"See. It's her."

The zombie girl looked back down again.

"Joe," I said, and the girl on the couch looked up again.

Dina looked upset with me. She turned to face me, cocked her head, and took me in with those clear, translucent eyes. There was a hum to her, a vibration—like a dropped guitar. "What is it you want?"

"I told you. I want to find my girlfriend."

She smiled patiently. She reached out and took my hand again in hers. "No. What do you *want*?"

"What?" My throat felt raw from the radiation. "I just want to talk to her."

"About what?"

"I'm sick," I said, and at that moment, the burning in my chest was overwhelming. "Cancer. I just found out a few weeks ago. Ozone sickness. Third stage. My application for gene therapy was turned down so they don't know how much time . . . I wanted to see Marci and . . ." I couldn't continue.

Dina stroked my hand with her slick white hand. "Apologize," she said.

"What?" I felt the air go out of me.

"You wanted to apologize? It's been two years and this is the first time you've come here," the black-haired woman said. And as she said it I knew it was true, and I wasn't sure anymore that the burning in my chest was coming from the radiation.

"You didn't even look for her," Dina continued, her voice entirely without judgment. "In fact, when she left, you were sort of . . . relieved. Weren't you? Relieved that she left before it got bad."

I tried to say no, but I couldn't speak.

"You would never have said it out loud, but you knew where it was going and you didn't know if you could do it. Take care of someone so . . . sick."

The room swirled as the pale woman spoke.

"Your anger was useful. You told yourself that she *wanted this*; that she *chose* this; that she *chose* to throw her life away."

I nodded weakly.

"But now you know . . . don't you?"

I could barely see her through my teary eyes.

"Now . . . you know what we know." Her voice went even lower. "That nobody *chooses*. That we're all sick. We're all here."

"I . . ." I looked at the ground. "I just wanted to tell her . . ."

"Tell her what?" Dina asked patiently.

I wept into my hands.

"Tell her what?" Dina whispered as she rubbed my shoulder. Finally, she turned to the other girl, sitting on the couch. "Marci?"

The zombie girl stood and grabbed the drugs off the table. "Tell her what?" Dina whispered.

"I'm here," I managed to say to the short-haired girl.

Dina nodded and smiled at me. Then she gently took my hand and pressed it into the other girl's pale hand. And Marci led me away.

THE NEW FRONTIER

I'M ON MY WAY to Vegas with my friend Bobby Rausch to rescue his stepsister from a life of prostitution.

It's August 2003: two weeks since I found out I failed the bar exam, six months since I got divorced, a year since I caught my wife with another man, eighteen months since she caught me cheating.

I'm on quite a streak.

Bobby's active duty in the air force, stationed at Fairchild; he gets us a lift on a transport out of Spokane. They strap us into jump seats in this flying boxcar and the thing lurches and rumbles and finally leaves the earth, Bobby giving a thumbs-up. I yell over the rumble of the plane, *Are you scared?*

In three weeks Bobby leaves for Iraq.

Scared? He flips up his sunglasses and grins at me. Bobby and I played football together at Mead High School, where we had one of those classic little-guy, big-guy friendships. But we hadn't seen each other in years when I bumped into him at a bar in Spokane. Bobby teaches at the air force survival school. It's the same thing he'll do in Iraq: teach airmen how to live on lice and tree bark, how to withstand torture if they're captured.

You know the only thing that scares me? Bobby says. *Going my whole life without getting the chance to prove myself.*

This is not the answer I would give.

Two hours after we take off, our plane crests the pocked red and tan bluffs and we bank hard over a baked floodplain, the desert blooming with shrimp-curled cul-de-sacs, a sprawl of earth-tone houses with swimming pools, and beyond, the glittering lights of Vegas.

That's when I throw up.

BOBBY'S PLAN in Vegas is to stay one step ahead of the wrecking ball—Sahara, Imperial Palace, New Frontier— *Goin' old strip*, Bobby Rausch calls it. It's also incredibly cheap, staying in hotels that are slated for demolition.

Bobby wanted me to come to Vegas because he thought he might need a lawyer. I keep telling him that I haven't actually passed the bar. *Oh if I know my old buddy Nick,* Bobby says, *he ain't gonna let that stop him from bein' a lawyer.*

Actually, I say, *failing the bar is* precisely *what stops you from being a lawyer.*

Well you can still give legal advice, right? he asks. *'Cause I might need some.* Then he adds, apropos of nothing, *Per se.*

What kind *of legal advice?* I ask. *Per se.*

Well, like whether or not I can kill this shithead who turned my sister into a whore.

I think about it for a minute. Then I tell Bobby my advice is to *not* kill the shithead who turned his stepsister into a whore.

See, he says.

ON THE STRIP, Rausch takes huge strides. I have to throw in a skip now and then just to keep up. At each hotel, he asks for the active-military discount. At each hotel, I lean over his shoulder and add: Two double beds, please.

Bobby's dream was to stay at the Sands and the Dunes, but those hotels have been torn down already, replaced by themed mega-resorts: Paris and the Venetian. So we stay at whatever old strip hotels *haven't* been blown up, like the New Frontier, which—according to the brochure—opened as a roadhouse in '42, reopened as the cowboy-themed Last Frontier in '55, became the space-themed New Frontier after Kennedy's 1960 convention speech (*We stand at the edge of a New Frontier—the frontier of unfulfilled hopes and dreams*), hosted Elvis's first Vegas performance in '69, and went back to being a cowboy place in the '70s.

Today, the New Frontier is a paint-chipped, dirty old shell of a building that takes up an entire block. Its eighty-foot sign advertises BIKINI BULL RIDING, $8.75 STEAK AND SHRIMP, and MUD WRESTLING along with COLD BEER AND DIRTY GIRLS. The hotel is scheduled to be demolished in a few months but the guests at the New Frontier don't look like they'll make it that long. Everywhere there are canes and walkers, oxygen machines and motorized wheelchairs. Even the *healthy* people move in clouds of cigarette smoke, women straining polyester, men in raggedy cutoffs slathering mayonnaise on foot-long hot dogs. It's as if the hotel were hosting a conference on adult onset diabetes.

Bobby goes to the room to shower, and I kill some time at a blackjack table. I sit between a man with one arm and a woman hooked to an oxygen machine. I look around to make sure we haven't checked into a VA hospital by mistake. Still, I win my first five hands, including two blackjacks. Then, on the sixth hand, I get a seventeen with the dealer showing a king. I hit, pull a four, and get twenty-one.

Wow, somebody's hot, says the woman next to me. Then she takes a hit from her oxygen machine.

THIS WHOLE TIME, I'm thinking, I really should tell Bobby why I decided to come on this trip.

EVERY NIGHT in Vegas, thousands of Mexican and Honduran immigrants stand along the street, handing out little playing cards with pictures of naked women on them. They snap the cards to get your attention. If you take a card and call the phone number on it, a stripper comes *direct to your hotel room.* Or a van picks you up and takes you to a brothel in the desert. Alongside the sexy women the cards feature some of the worst ad copy you've ever seen: *Nothing BUTT the best for you* and *Why not CUM see me tonight—*

It's hard for me to imagine a human being stupid enough to need those nasty puns capitalized, but I suppose they're out there.

These snapper cards are the reason Bobby and I have come. Six weeks ago, one of Rausch's fellow air force instructors returned from Vegas with a handful of these cards; on one of them was a photo of Bobby's stepsister, Lisa. Bobby called the number on the card, but that particular company was out of business.

I was dubious that it was Lisa until I saw the photo. It's her all right. In the picture, she wears a white thong and is bending forward, bare-chested, little stars covering her nipples. Her card reads: *Want me in your room in 30 minutes?* Like a pizza. You could just see, on her hip, a little Panther tattoo. Our high school mascot. I remember when she got that tattoo. Rausch and I were seniors; she was a sophomore. Rausch punched his locker when he heard about it. Then he punched the poor kid who'd seen her hip tattoo.

Rausch's dad divorced Lisa's mom a year after that, but Bobby continued to call Lisa his sister. He'd heard that she moved to Las Vegas and that she was dating *a porno photographer*. She told her family she was in real estate.

There has been a downturn in housing prices, I offer helpfully.

I FIRST met Lisa when I was a junior in high school and she was a freshman. I'd gone to Bobby's house to see if he wanted to hang out. The Rausches were a big blended family, one kid on each side when the parents got married, and two babies between them. That day Lisa was in a lawn chair on the porch, wearing the tiniest pair of shorts, reading a magazine, and flipping a sandal up and down with her toe. *I sure like your Camaro, Nick*, she called down from the porch.

I told her it was a Cavalier.

Really? She smiled. *Why so cavalier, Nick?*

I could not think of a thing to say. So often around Lisa I couldn't think of a thing to say.

Bobby's not here, she said. *I'm the only one home.* She flipped a sandal up and caught it with her toes. *Still feeling cavalier . . . Nick?* The way she hung on my name (*Nick-ah*) I swear it was the sexiest thing I'd ever heard.

Lisa was my first. There was something teasing and irresistible about her. We had to sneak around because she was so young and because Bobby was so overprotective. She'd leave the basement window open at night, and I'd crawl in, lower myself onto the air-hockey table, and go into her bedroom. She always kept her socks on for some reason. The sex was amazing, although, to be fair, I was seventeen and sex was pretty much amazing by definition. Still, this thing between us only lasted a couple of months. She was the one to end it; I think she got bored.

Rausch knows none of this.

A FEW WEEKS before we graduated from high school, I heard a rumor from my sister's friend: that Lisa Rausch had gotten an abortion. It was quite a while after we finished sleeping together. So it probably wasn't mine. She was fifteen. I never said a word to her about it. This is another thing Bobby knows nothing about.

IN VEGAS, Bobby insists that we *stick and move, stick and move.* When I ask why, he says, *Because when you're asking the kinds of questions we're asking, it's not long before the people you're looking for . . . start looking for you.*

I can't imagine the questions we're asking causing anyone to look for us. In fact, for the first three days, we only ask the one question: *Have you seen this girl?* We stagger up and down the strip asking our one question, collecting nudie cards from snappers.

Sometimes Bobby wears his flight jacket. People come up to him and thank him for his service.

How's the war going over there? people will ask.

About to get a lot better, Bobby will say. Then he'll wink.

One day, out of nowhere, Rausch starts calling us the Dream Team.

The Dream Team's days begin at 5:30 A.M. It doesn't matter what time we go to bed, Rausch wakes me at 5:30, yelling, *Let's go, Little Buddy.* We go to breakfast, I gamble a little (I'm still on my strange winning streak.) while Bobby hangs out in the room, then we walk to a new hotel, take a nap, start drinking, gamble some more, eat at a buffet, and spend the night collecting snapper cards, looking through the pictures of strippers until, well after midnight, we stagger back to our room. This is when Rausch becomes philosophical. *Ain't no one I'd rather have at my side, you know that, Little Buddy? You and me, we're the Dream Team, last of the heroes.*

It's August. During the day the temperature hits 110; at night it drops into the high 90s. We move in an endless stream of drunken losers from casino to casino, past the snappers wearing their Day-Glo T-shirts advertising GIRLS DIRECT TO YOUR ROOM and TWO GIRLS FOR THE PRICE OF ONE. Rausch takes a card from each one and rifles through them, looking for Lisa. Every once in a while he shows the snappers the old card with Lisa's picture on it. *You seen this girl?*

Si, say the snappers. And they thumb through their own cards until they find a blonde they think looks like Rausch's sister.

This one, she prettier, eh Boss? says one snapper. He holds up a card showing another beautiful blonde.

I don't want prettier, Rausch says. *I want my sister.*

He . . . doesn't mean that, I say.

Sometimes, Rausch goes crazy non-sequitur bad-cop on the snappers. *I'm gonna give you the gist here, pal*, he'll say, towering over some poor Salvadoran. Or *I don't think you're understanding my gravity.* Or *Two choices, Paco: number one, the INS runs you back to Tijuana, or B., you tell me who operates your little . . . operation.*

But the snappers have no idea who operates their operation. They line up in a vacant lot somewhere and get their cards from some guy in a pickup truck. We might as well grab a migrant fruit picker out of a Florida peach field and demand the phone number of the CEO of Del Monte.

AFTER DAYS of grilling snappers and getting nothing but a stack of nudie cards, Bobby turns our attention to the strip clubs. He shows me a thick roll of singles. *This is the only currency these sleaze merchants understand.*

I say that's probably because it's actual currency.

He slides dollars one at a time into girls' G-strings. He shows the dancers the old card with Lisa's picture on it. *My partner and I are looking for this girl.*

We're not . . . that kind of partners, I point out helpfully.

The strippers don't know Lisa, or they know a girl who looks like her, or sure, her name is Destiny or Tanya or Flemisha, or they know a girl who looks like her dancing at a club in Phoenix and if we want a lap dance they can tell us more.

Rausch buys lap dances in every place, but he never seems to learn anything. He tells the strippers on break that he's come to rescue his sister. I think he expects them to be moved by his gallantry, but they never react and we end up sitting quietly, watching girls swing their implants around poles. I'd guess we've seen about fifty naked girls. Rausch is running out of singles. My balls feel like they're going to explode.

It takes away from my sense of chivalry, having a constant erection. It's been a year since Amanda and I split, and I haven't exactly been what one might call *active*, unless one counts oneself. And I can't even do *that* on this trip.

But Rausch *can* do *that*. All the time. He goes into the bathroom and does *that* any time he pleases, even with me on the other side of the door. In fact, he rubs one off at least twice a day, quickly and efficiently, morning and night, like brushing his teeth.

I wonder if this is one of the advantages of military training.

After masturbating he always climbs in his bed and wants to talk. *First we find Lisa. Then, when I get back from Iraq, you and me should get a place together. A house or something. You and me on the rampage in Spokane? You kidding me?*

I breathe heavily, trying not to overdo it by fake-snoring.

You and me, we're a dying breed, Little Buddy.

MY ONLY respite is blackjack. Rausch hates the game; he prefers slots. At a worn five-dollar table, I asked the dealer what's going to replace the New Frontier. He shrugs, but another player, a woman with an eye patch, tells me, *The Montreux. Swiss-themed. With a 450-foot observation wheel, like in London.* The woman tells me she's from Orem, Utah, and that she has left an abusive husband. She pats the eye patch and drags her cigarette and nods at the dealer for a hit. She busts a fourteen and waves her hand away. I stand on a nineteen, and the dealer busts. *Stupid game*, she says.

She's right. It is stupid. All of it. And when Bobby comes back from watching bikini bull riding, I tell him so. *What are we doing?* I ask. *We're just wasting our time. We're never gonna find Lisa this way.*

You read my mind, partner, he says.

A WEEK before I failed the bar exam, I saw my ex-wife's engagement announcement in the newspaper. The guy she's marrying, the guy I caught her with, is eleven years older than me. They're getting married at the Davenport Hotel. They're going to St. Thomas for their honeymoon. I'd never seen Ame-

lia look as happy as she did in that picture. I'm not saying that
was why I failed the bar exam. Or maybe I am. I don't know.

APPARENTLY WHEN a casino like the New Frontier is set
for demolition, they don't bother cleaning the carpets anymore. The array of stains is mind-blowing. *Listen*, Bobby says
as we walk back to our room, *I know you're getting unpatient, but
we're close. I can feel it. We're making some people very nervous.*

I can't imagine anyone getting nervous, other than me,
as back in the room Rausch finishes his push-ups, grabs the
lotion, and heads for the bathroom to jerk off. It sounds like
someone plunging a toilet in there.

HOW WELL do you really know your old high school
friends? At Mead, I just thought he was a jock, a guy who
listened to country music and knew people who could buy
us beer. I'm finding out now my old buddy is a creature of
strange habits. Twice a day, Rausch does eighty push-ups and
eighty sit-ups. He wears extremely tight, silky T-shirts. He
picks his teeth with a pocketknife after meals and cleans his
toes while he watches TV. He never seems to fully exhale. I
imagine he has oxygen in his lungs from 1990. He shaves his
balding head and runs his hand constantly over the ridge on
top, which looks like the drive train of a pickup. He'll never
get married because *I don't need no ring to get no pussy.* I think
he's unaware of the double negative. He tells me he has four
girlfriends back in Spokane, two of whom are married. He
liked married women because *they're used to being fucked bad.*
Again, I don't know if this is preferable because he plans to
have bad sex with them or because his superior sex impresses
them. When I ask for clarification, he just stares at me.

He seems to like having a sidekick, but is completely unin-
terested in my life. He only asks about my divorce once, as we
lean out over the strip in the Margaritaville bar. I'm drunk,
and I tell him the whole boring story: how we got married,
how we got jobs in different cities, how we both cheated in
our separate cities, and how, by the time I made it to Portland, where Amelia was living, she was already in love with
this older guy. When I finish, Bobby is quiet. He stares at the
flow of drunks below us, and finally says, *Bitch*.

I think you missed the point, I say.

Here's the point. And he jabs at me with his beer. *You and me?
It takes a different sort of gal to tame us. We're desperados. We ain't
exactly your average husband material.*

I WOULD just quit and go home . . . but the thing is: I keep
winning. In fact, I can't seem to lose. Blackjack mostly. But
also Let It Ride. And a Texas Hold 'Em Bonus game that
offers the worst table odds in Vegas, but which I keep hitting
like it's a gumball machine. After a week, I'm up six grand.

Rausch won't take a dime from me, though, won't let me
pay for the room . . . nothing. *Can't let you do that, Little Buddy*,
he says. *This here's my fight*. He explains that he saved up his
leave for this trip, and he has one more week—*damned if I'm
gonna rest while my sister is having her boobies sold off one at a time*.

I have no idea what this could mean. Finally, I can't take
it anymore. On the eighth day, I tell him I'm leaving the next
morning, that we're never going to find her just going to strip
clubs and collecting snapper cards.

Bobby is hurt. He's quiet for a moment, and then he sighs,
climbs out of bed, and begins getting dressed.

Look, I say, *I'm sorry, but it's true.*

He walks out the door. And the next thing I know he's shaking me awake by the foot. *Wake up. Come on.*

I sit up. The clock on the nightstand reads 3:15. I ask where we're going.

Where we should've gone from day one, he says, *the belly of the viper.*

I follow Bobby Rausch downstairs. In the cab turnout we climb aboard a minivan driven by a Russian guy in a sweat suit. There are six of us behind the driver in the van—two long-haired blond guys who looked like the terrorist twins from *Die Hard* (Rausch watches them carefully) and two giggling-drunk businessmen in suits. The van heads out into the desert. Rausch is uncharacteristically quiet. He stares out his window. At four in the morning, there's nothing out here but our headlights.

The brothel is called the Pony Palace. There don't appear to be any Ponies. The Palace is a small metal building with a half-dozen doublewides flanking it.

We open the door and a bell rings as we step inside a sad little bar. The bartender draws us ten-dollar beers. I pay for the beers, the least I can do. On the ride out I assumed that Rausch had some information that Lisa was at this particular brothel, but when the hookers come out—summoned by a bell—Lisa isn't there. Rausch chooses a waif: thin and pale with dark hair, a girl who has either her original breasts or a bad plastic surgeon. Bobby pays three hundred dollars for an hour of *questioning.* I sit on a couch next to the taller of the two businessmen, who has cold feet.

FOR SOME REASON, the reluctant businessman and I feel the need to explain ourselves. The tall businessman says, *My daughter is twenty-six, and I just keep thinking: these girls are* someone's daughters.

I say that I'm not over my ex-wife. And as soon as I say it, I realize it's true. And I feel like crying.

AT DAWN we get back into the minivan: the one sated businessman; the one who didn't want to sleep with someone's daughter; the two satisfied blond Fabio terrorists, both of whom chose black women; me; Rausch; and his waifish whore, whose name turns out to be Meilani. She has a backpack and a suitcase.

Can she just leave like that? I whisper to Rausch.

I hope to hell someone tries to stop her, Rausch says loudly to the room.

Meilani explains to me that *they can't* stop her. The girls are independent contractors who pay a percentage to the house. After describing other fascinating aspects of her business on the drive back to Vegas (*You have to pay for your own STD tests.*), Meilani goes to sleep on Rausch's shoulder.

I'm glad Bobby has found someone to rescue. Now I can go home to Spokane.

Back at the New Frontier, the air conditioning is out. It's ninety-two degrees in our room. Meilani curls up on top of Rausch's bed in a pair of panties.

I pack my things, say, *Best of luck, man. You keep your head down over there. Come back in one piece.*

Rausch is stunned. *What? You're leaving? But we're getting so close. Did you see how nervous we made those people at the Pony Palace?*

I start for the door, but then I turn. I tell him that Lisa was the first girl I ever slept with. I say that was why I had agreed to come. Because I felt I owed her.

Bobby blinks twice. Then, no blinking for a while. Then another blink. *When?*

End of our junior year, I say. I tell him about the open basement window.

Bobby looked disgusted. *Those weren't even egress windows.*

I don't feel qualified to address the window size. I turn to leave.

So, he asks, *was everyone fucking my sister?*

Can we get some quesadillas? Meilani asks from the bed.

I BOOK A FLIGHT out the next morning and check into my own room at the New Frontier. The air conditioning works in my room. I spread out on the bed and think about Amelia.

When I first got to Portland, I wanted so badly for it to work out between us. I felt awful about sleeping around on her while I was in law school, but I was certain I was done with all of that, and that we could start over. I opened the phone book and found a florist near her apartment, walked there and ordered a bouquet of tulips, her favorite. The clerk said they already had her name and address in their computer. They wouldn't tell me who had been sending her flowers.

THERE'S A PHONE BOOK in the drawer of my room at the New Frontier. On a whim, I open it. First I try Lisa Rausch. Nothing. Then I remember Rausch's stepmother's maiden name was Heitmaker. So I look up Lisa Heitmaker.

I find a listing for Heitmaker Realty.

I call the number.

This is Lisa.

I tell her it's Nick.

She's quiet for a second and then she laughs. *Come on. Really?* She laughs again. *Did you drive down here in your Cavalier, Nick?*

We meet at the food court of the Riviera. Lisa looks older than the photo on the card. Her hair is short now, brown with streaks of blond. She's incredibly tan and wears a loose-fitting sundress. She's also six months pregnant. The father is her new boyfriend, a Vegas developer. *It's complicated*, she says. *He's older. And sort of married. For now.*

I stare at her little pregnant bulge. I say I have to ask her something. *In high school, you had an abortion.*

Is that a question? she asks. Then she says she doesn't know who got her pregnant. *Maybe you. Or Billy DiPino.* She laughs uneasily. *You came all this way to ask about that? Don't they have phones where you live?*

Actually, I say, *I came with Bobby.*

Her smile fades. *Wait. You're here with Bobby?*

Yeah, we came to rescue you from a life of prostitution.

She explains how she'd ended up on a stripper card. Years ago, she did, in fact, date a sleazy photographer. He convinced her to model for some topless photos, and after they broke up he sold the pictures without getting her to sign a release. *You guys do know that the women in the pictures are models? They aren't the actual girls who come to your room. Right?*

I shrug as if to say, *Of course we knew that*, although it hadn't occurred to me.

Lisa was working for a real estate broker when her picture showed up on the snapper cards. At first she was devastated. But then, with the help of her new boyfriend's lawyer, she sued. The company that produced the cards, a big LA advertising firm, quickly settled, and Lisa invested half of the money in the boyfriend's new development project—a neighborhood of Spanish stuccos abutting the desert. She invested the bulk of the proceeds from that project into two others. Lisa is doing very well.

I ask if she could call Bobby and tell him that she's okay. I say it would mean a lot to him.

I can't do that, Nick, she says. Then she narrows her eyes. *Wait. You don't know why our parents split up, do you?* And then she tells me the rest of the story, the part I feel stupid for not knowing—or for not guessing. There are apparently no limits to the delusions of old desperados like us. We *are* indeed a kind of Dream Team: Bobby and me.

She was twelve. He was fifteen. They were home alone that summer. It might have been perfectly natural if their parents weren't married. But when her mom found out, she freaked out and got them all into family counseling. Lisa quickly got over it, but Bobby wouldn't leave her alone. For the next four years he sulked. He beat up her boyfriends. He followed her. After their parents divorced, Lisa had to get a restraining order against Bobby.

I CALL Rausch's cell phone, hoping he won't pick up, so I can just leave a message. But he answers on the first ring.

Meilani? he asks, his voice wavering, desperate.

I say it's Nick.

Nick? Oh. Hey. His voice became sturdy again. *Shit. She cleaned out my wallet. I woke up from a nap and Meilani was gone.*

I HAVE this theory, that this will be the only city that future archaeologists find, Las Vegas. The dry climate will preserve it all and teams of scientists in the year 5000 will carefully sweep and scrape away the sand to find pyramids and castles and replicas of the Eiffel Tower and the New York skyline and stripper poles and snapper cards and these future archaeologists will re-create our entire culture based solely on this one shallow and cynical little shithole.

We can complain all we want that this city doesn't represent us. We can say, *Yes, but I hated Las Vegas.* Or *I only went there once.* Well, I'm sure not all Romans reveled in the torture-fests at the Colosseum either, but there it is.

That afternoon, I walk. The sun presides over crowded sidewalks; streets course with stretch hummers; shadows reach from the big facades fronting all those giant, bland block-and-steel boxes. Beneath the streets, gladiators sharpen their spears; lions await.

I MEET Bobby in front of the New Frontier and give him five hundred dollars. I offer to give him more, but he says it's all he needs. In fact, he tells me, he could've easily made it home without the loan. I don't doubt it. I imagine him walking across the desert, sucking water from cactus roots, and cooking cockroaches in his boiling saliva.

I tell him that I found Lisa. That she's fine, that she isn't a prostitute, that the picture on the snapper card was a mistake. I also repeat what she asked me to tell him: that under no circumstances should he try to contact her.

Good, good. Very good. He acts as if he didn't hear this last part. *How'd you find her, anyway?*

I tell him I looked in the telephone book.

He shakes his head admiringly, as if I've just described some kind of global search involving advanced GPS and DNA databases. *See,* he says, *that's exactly why I brought you in on this one.* This one: as if it's one of our many *cases* together. Then he asks, *How'd she look?*

I promised not to tell him about the baby. *Fat*, I say.

He nods and looks off into the distance. Flexes. Inhales. Wrinkles his brow. He has five more days before he has to report. *There are certain people you feel like are supposed to be in your life forever, you know? Like, there's been some mistake . . .* then he sighs. *What do you say we go get that wife of yours back?*

She's getting remarried, I tell him for at least the third time.

Oh. He nods. *What are you gonna do now?*

Stick and move, I say.

THEN BOBBY RAUSCH smiles and stares down the strip. We are standing outside the New Frontier, beneath that eighty-foot sign. The street shimmers. Sweat beads Rausch's head like a newly waxed car. He looks up at the sign. *They always tear down the good shit,* he says. *It's always the end of the legacy, ain't it?*

I tell him I can't argue with that.

Then Rausch holds out his hand. I'm not thrilled to touch it after all the pleasure he's given himself, but I take it and he pulls me in tight for a hug. *We did it, man. They said the Dream Team couldn't do it, but hell if we didn't come down here and find her.*

We say good-bye then, and I start back down the strip. The snappers flick their cards at me: A girl in your room in forty minutes!

GOD, I ache for those girls.

A LONG BLOCK AWAY, I glance back. Bobby Rausch is still standing there, beneath the New Frontier sign. He is a head taller than the crowd around him, and for just a moment he is framed against the brash, spread-out skyline, staring off, maybe at something beyond the strip, beyond bikini bull riding and dirty-girl mud-wrestling, beyond stripper cards and the last cowboy and archaeologists and his generation's war, beyond even the myth of an $8.95 steak-and-shrimp dinner. And suddenly Bobby Rausch is moving again, not with our old meandering strip-stroll, but with real purpose, perhaps with the stride of a changed man, a man headed for a new realm of honest insight and humility, a man finally making his way out of this frontier of stale and unfulfilled dreams.

Or maybe he's just headed for the Flamingo.

THE BRAKES

TOMMY DROVE away from Ken's funeral, kid next to him on the bench seat, kicking at the air in front of the glove box.

—Do you gotta do a funeral when you die?

—No.

—If nobody's gonna be there but four people they shouldn't do one.

—Army paid for it, Tommy said.

—Did you like him?

No, Tommy thought. —Yeah, he said.

—Were you sad when your mom married him?

Yeah, Tommy thought. —No, he said.

—Then your mom died. It wasn't a question so Tommy didn't answer it. The kid's sneakers kept kicking air. —If Jeff marries Mom he'd be my stepdad.

—Yeah.

Tommy could only get the morning off, so he brought the kid back to work with him. —I'll get you some popcorn, and you can watch the TV.

—Okay, the kid said. Tommy pulled in back of the garage. The old racist lady's Lincoln was jacked up in bay three.

Inside, Miguel was popping lug-nuts with the pneumatic. Tommy looked over, through the window into the bullpen. The old racist lady sat staring out the window with a cup of coffee. Hunched back. Hair like old wire. She watched Miguel suspiciously. She saw Tommy through the window, sat up, and waved.

Miguel nodded at the raised car. —Tires *and* brakes, dude. It's slow as shit so Andy said to give her the works.

Tommy wiggled into his coveralls.

—Where's he at?

—Andy? He went to get Taco Bell. I don't think he knew you was gonna be back.

Tommy went into the bullpen, the kid a step behind. —I'm glad you're here, said the old racist lady. —That wetback makes me nervous.

—Mrs. Gerraghty . . .

—Before my husband died, he said, Always take care of the tires and brakes. Don't ever let them put you on junk.

Tommy glanced out the window toward bay three, where Miguel was watching him.

The old racist lady leaned forward as if sharing a secret. —I used to go to the garage by our house. But they have a colored fella working there.

—I know. You told me.

—Bad enough having a beaner work on it, but Carl would die all over again if I let a nigger anywhere near the Lincoln.

Tommy felt the kid flinch next to him. He grabbed the boy's hand. —Mrs. Gerraghty, I wish you wouldn't talk like that.

She laughed. —Oh, I don't mean anything by it. They call each other that, you know.

Tommy walked his kid over to the popcorn in the back of the waiting room. —She's a stupid old lady.

Kid nodded. —We did a thing about Martin Lufer King at school.

Tommy got him settled in front of the TV. He put it on the public station. Puppets. Then he went to the counter. Her work order was sitting there. Andy's handwriting. Eight hundred sixty bucks. Goddamn. Tommy walked over and sat next to her. —Mrs. Gerraghty, remember you came in last week, and I said you didn't need tires?

She looked past him, into the bay. —I wish *you* would do the work, or the other nice white man.

—You said you have a niece, right? Over in Post Falls?

She made a face. —My sister's girl. She's fat. Her daughter looks like a mongoloid.

—You were going to bring me her phone number.

—She eats enough for five. I have no respect for that.

—What about her last name? You know that?

—She married this man Geller. I think he's queer. No wonder they had a mongoloid.

Tommy went to the counter. He tried information, and on the second Geller in Post Falls, Tommy got the woman's niece. —Your aunt's here buying tires.

—Senile old bitch, the niece said. Then she hung up.

Andy pulled up in back then. Tommy walked out to meet him. Andy got out of his truck with two bags of Taco Bell.

—Andy.

—Sorry, man. I didn't know if you'd ate or not.

—Let's just rotate her tires, Tommy said.

—Who, old racist lady? He smiled.

—Come on. It's only been three weeks. Six since we did her brakes.

And three weeks before that, Tommy thought. And six

weeks before that. Of course, they didn't really do the brakes.
Just jacked the car and popped the wheels. Swung hammers
and pretended to use screw drivers. Sometimes all three of
them pretended to work on it together, grabbing random tools,
making faces to each other, turning their backs to laugh, old
racist lady watching from the bullpen.

The three-week-old tires Andy sold online.

—It's enough, Tommy said.

Andy waved him off, walked past him with the Taco Bell
bags.

Tommy was surprised to hear himself. —I'll call the cops.

Andy stopped. He turned. Gave a little smile. Took a half
step toward him.

—Dad, can I turn it to Nickelodeon?

They both turned and saw Tommy's kid standing in the
doorway. In his good jeans and shirt for the funeral.

They stood there. Andy. Tommy. Tommy's kid. Tommy
aware of his own breathing. His kid's eyes on him. He must
look so big from down there, Tommy thought. The way Ken
did, fucking Ken, holding a beer or a belt, always pissed at
Tommy's mom, at him sometimes, at the whole goddamn
world mostly. Tommy stood his ground.

Finally Andy scratched his head, sighed, and walked to
the door of bay three. He yelled to Miguel. —Rotate her tires.
Fluids and belts.

He held up one of the bags. —And your fuckin' food's
here, Miguel.

Andy gave Tommy a sideways glance as he walked back
into the bullpen. —Good news, Mrs. Gerraghty. Your brakes
look okay after all.

Tommy took his kid back to the TV in the waiting room.

Turned it to Nickelodeon. There was a cartoon about this little genius kid. There was a cartoon like that when he was a kid, but Tommy couldn't remember the name of it. He felt tired. Slumped next to his kid on the couch. Looked down on the cow-licked swoop of the kid's hair.

—You know it don't matter who your mom marries, right? I ain't goin' nowhere.

The kid looked up. He offered his dad some popcorn.

THE WOLF AND THE WILD

1

THEY FANNED out in the brown grass along Highway 2 like geese in a loose V, eight men in white coveralls and orange vests picking up trash. In the center, in the hump between lanes, Wade McAdam found himself explaining futures trading to a drug dealer named Ricky.

"Wait," Ricky said. "So you're just betting on whether the price goes up? You need a fuckin' finance degree for *that*?" He grabbed something with his trash-picker and showed it to Wade: a shit-filled diaper. Then he flicked it back into the weeds. "Sick."

Wade snagged the diaper and put it in his bag. "Yeah, but the wheat, the stock, the energy, whatever—it never changes hands. The *thing* is beside the point. You're selling a contract. You're selling the instrument itself—"

"Wait, what?"

Wade shielded the sun from his eyes. "See, the underlying asset can be anything: a hedge fund, an interest rate. Hell, you can sell futures on futures. The thing doesn't matter. All you're doing is spreading risk. You make money no matter what." Wade smiled at the irony of saying this while wearing a prison jumpsuit. "You know, within a certain algorithmic range."

"Goddamn it, Beans, you totally lost me."

Wade didn't know why the men called him Beans.

Ricky grabbed a Taco Bell bag with his picker, flicked it into his garbage sack. "You're like them scientists on TV explaining black holes. More you talk, less I get."

2

AT GROUP, Wade just listened.

Ricky always got emotional in the big circle. He twitched and wept and said he could see the "patterns I been chained to my whole life." The social worker in the wheelchair asked if that meant Ricky was "ready to go straight now."

"Oh fuck, definitely," Ricky said.

After group Wade asked Ricky if he was really going to quit dealing drugs.

"Oh, that ain't what I'm here for, Beans," Ricky said. "I diddled my neighbor's kid."

3

WADE DIDN'T even know they still made Fanta, but there were two empty cans in the weeds along the highway.

"How'd you get caught, Beans?" Ricky asked.

Wade paused over a cigarette pack. Pall Malls. Did they still make Pall Malls? This stretch of highway was a time machine. "One of the partners had a girlfriend," Wade said. "Anna. After his wife found out, I started seeing Anna. Next audit, my partner pointed out some internal controls that I'd let slip. Trust-account funds that had mingled into my . . ." Wade stopped and stared up at the sky. "Black holes," he said.

"How much you take?" Ricky asked.

Wade looked back down at the sandy tufts of grass along the highway, at the line of orange-vested men with their garbage-picking spears and trash-bag shields. "Not enough," he said.

4

ANOTHER TIME Ricky said, "Don't be so hard on your-self, Beans. Everybody up in this shit for some kind of greed or fucking."

5

WADE'S LAWYERS said they could get him transferred back to Seattle for community service, but he didn't want some old client seeing him cleaning pigeon shit in Pioneer Square. His kids wanted nothing to do with him. And until the divorce was finalized, he didn't even know which house to go to.

No, he said, he'd just do his community service in Spo-kane.

At the hearing, Densmore got the judge to agree to shorter probation in exchange for a steeper fine and Wade's involve-ment in a community-service pilot program. Wade had never worked with the criminal side of the firm before; Densmore was crudely efficient, brusque even, as if this business was beneath him. The hearing took all of four minutes. It was between the lawyers. While they talked at the bench, Wade looked down at the white socks he had on beneath the suit Densmore's secretary had brought for him.

"We'll see you back in Seattle in six weeks," Densmore said when it was over. He closed his briefcase. "Now if you don't mind, I'm going to try to catch the four PM flight."

Back at Geiger, Wade looked for twitchy Ricky to say good-bye, but apparently he'd been caught flashing one of the female prisoners on the federal side of the fence and shipped back to the sex farm at Shelton.

6

REAL ESTATE was practically free in Spokane. Wade had known that, of course, but it seemed somehow profane to be standing in a fully furnished, two-bedroom downtown loft that went for half the monthly price of his sailboat moorage. He walked from room to room, the property manager a step behind. She explained that Wade would need to provide "bank statements, pay stubs, references, that sort of thing." In the kitchen, Wade used her laptop to call up his personal checking account. The property manager said not to worry about the references and the pay stubs.

She suggested a nice restaurant a few blocks away, and Wade went alone, took a seat at the bar. He had a scotch and water, his first drink in sixteen months. He closed his eyes as he drank it. His counselor at Geiger had once asked him if booze wasn't perhaps "the first knot in your life." How to answer something like that? It was knots all the way down.

"Want me to pour the next one straight down your gullet?" the bartender asked.

Wade looked down at his empty glass, then up at the bartender. She was in her thirties, slight and attractive, with short black hair. She smiled at him, a little warily. Then she filled him up again.

"No sense dirtying a glass if you're going to inhale it," she said.

He tipped it, barely let the whiskey touch his lips, then put it down.

"Attaboy," she said.

7

THE VOLUNTEER coordinator was a thin woman with a flesh-colored eye patch and an atrophied left arm that curled into her breast like a hawk's claw. Wade wondered if she'd had a stroke.

"This is a very controversial pilot program," she explained. "We don't typically let ex-cons work with children. But our test results call for drastic measures, and since you white-collar assholes are the least likely to volunteer, we're targeting a few hand-picked, non-violent offenders to supply supervised, one-on-one tutoring." She closed his file. "Now, this program is my baby, and I'd really hate to lose my job, so I'd consider it a personal favor if you could refrain from having kids bring you their mom's checkbooks."

"I'll try," Wade said.

She slid a contract across the table. "You check in at the school office every time. If you go walking alone down a hallway or contact a student outside school, anything like that? Start some Ponzi lunch-money scheme? It's back to Geiger for you, my friend, and my little program dies. Understand?"

Wade nodded.

"Four hours a day, four days a week," she went on. "Two days you'll work at a high school, two days at an elementary school. Sophomores and second-graders. We're assigning you to two very good, veteran teachers. Any questions?"

"I didn't get your name."

She seemed uncomfortable with this and looked away from him with her good eye. "Sheila," she said.

"Well, Sheila," he said, "thanks for this opportunity. I'll do my best."

8

MEGAN'S MOUTH hung as if on a loose hinge, her eyes half-lidded. She blinked, sighed, stared at the page, at the equation, at oblivion. Wade had to fight to keep from reaching over and gently closing her jaw.

"Come on, Megan. We just went over this. The coefficients are . . ."

"Ni-i-ine," she said, "and . . . fi-i-ive?"

"That's right. And the variables."

"Are the letters?"

"Right, although technically a letter could be a coefficient too, if there're no assumed variables."

"What?"

"Nothing. Sorry. So how would you go about solving this?"

Megan looked over her shoulder, back into the classroom, where Mr. Watkins was going over more complex equations on the board. Then she leaned in closer to Wade. "Were you really in jail?"

"Let's just concentrate on these problems, okay?"

"Did you do a murder or something?"

"No," Wade said. "I didn't pay attention in algebra."

9

THIS BOY Drew kept trying to crawl up in Wade's lap to read.

They were on a couch just outside the office; Wade looked up at the secretary and shrugged, as if to assure her that he hadn't put the kid on his lap, that he wasn't a pervert. But the secretary was giving some other kid his Ritalin from a drawer in her desk and didn't seem to notice. "Why don't you sit over here," Wade said, and he gently moved the boy.

Drew was tiny for a second-grader. At first Wade wondered if he'd just forgotten how small seven-year-olds were, since his own kids were seventeen and nineteen now, but then he saw Drew with his class and the boy was a head smaller than everyone else. He moved his tiny index finger along each word as he read, as if each one was a story unto itself.

The boy brought the same book for their one-hour reading session every time. *The Wolf and the Wild.*

"Don't you want to bring another book?" Wade finally asked him.

Drew considered this for a moment. "But I don't know what's in those other books."

"Isn't that the fun, finding out?"

Drew looked dubious.

10

"IS IT the . . . associative law?"

Wade pointed to the problem again. "No, it's the other one."

"Associative?"

"No, you just said associative, J'mar. It's the other one."

J'mar stared at him.

"Dist . . ." Wade said, his eyebrows arching.

J'mar stared.

"Distrib . . ."

J'mar stared.

"Dis . . . trib . . . u . . . tive."

"Distributive?" J'mar said, as if he'd just come up with it.

"Nice," Wade said.

11

THE BARTENDER'S name was Sonya. She was married. Wade was a little disappointed, but also a little relieved.

"I like working with the little kids," Wade said, "but the high schoolers are stupid. Distracted."

"You had to go to prison to learn that?" Sonya refilled his whiskey.

"On the bright side, I *have* figured out how to fix the American educational system. End it at sixth grade."

"Brilliant. Then what?"

"Lock them up in empty factories, give them all the Red Bull, condoms, and nachos they want, pipe in club music, and check back when they're twenty-five. Anyone still alive, we send to grad school." Wade pushed his glass forward. "How's that for a campaign platform?"

"Hate to break it to you," said Sonya, "but I'm pretty sure you can't run for office."

12

IN *The Wolf and the Wild*, a little boy lives on a farm without any brothers and sisters. Every night he hears a wolf howling. One day he sees the animal at the edge of their farm.

That night his mother makes round steak. The boy hates round steak. He sneaks it into his lap and then into his pocket, and later that night he leaves it at the edge of the farm for the wolf. Every night after that, he takes some food out to the edge of the farm. Then one day he gets lost in the woods.

After a few hours, he sees the wolf in the distance, and eventually it leads him home. The boy tells his parents how the wolf saved him, but they only laugh, in a kindly way. "You probably just imagined it," they tell him.

On the last five pages of the book there are no words at all. The boy is older, and he's going for a walk with a sack lunch. In one panel he walks through the wheat field. In the next, he walks through the woods. In the next, he comes across the wolf. In the final panel, he is lying back with his head on the curled-up animal, staring up at the sky while he and the wolf share his lunch. This was Drew's favorite part of the book.

"And that's the end," Drew said every time they got to that last page. Then he'd sigh, look up, put his hand on Wade's arm, and smile.

13

WADE ROLLED over and watched Sonya put on her bra. She wouldn't look back at him.

"The funny thing is, it wasn't that bad, being in prison," he said. "They put you with other nonviolent offenders, the white-collars and the frauds. Stone liars. It wasn't until work-release that I even met any *real* criminals. And even they were okay. You think it's all going to be beatings in the yard and gang rapes in the shower, but it's just a bunch of fucked-up guys at summer camp."

She stood and zipped her skirt. She looked miserable. "I can't do this," she said.

He leaned back and stared up at the ceiling of his apartment. "The only thing I could never figure out was why they called me 'Beans.' I thought they meant that I spilled the beans. But I didn't. Who was I going to testify against? It was all me."

"I won't be able to live with myself," she said.

14

"AND THAT'S the end," Drew said. He closed *The Wolf and the Wild*, put his hand on Wade's arm, and smiled.

15

WADE KEPT detailed reports on all the kids, the sophomores and the second graders: Megan's progress in algebra, Tania's struggles with geometry, J'mar and his quick mind for figures but inability to grasp concepts. The way DeAndre was working on sounding out longer words and Marco was anticipating story elements and creating voices for characters. And, of course, Drew.

"Most of these kids have no parental involvement in school," Sheila told him one day at the office, as she looked over his notes. "These classes are ninety to ninety-five percent free and reduced lunch. Every kid is essentially living in poverty. Single-parent homes are the best case; a lot of them live with aunts, grandmothers, foster parents, random people."

He always wanted to ask Sheila what had happened to her arm and her eye.

"But I have to say, you're doing great with them," she said.

"Thank you," Wade said.

16

WADE FINALLY talked Drew into bringing another book, *Dog Day*. The boy tried to crawl up in Wade's lap again, but this time the secretary was watching. She opened her mouth to say something, and Wade nodded at her and gently pushed Drew back onto the couch. His own son, Michael, had been a lap-reader, and Wade felt a tug of regret just thinking about that little boy, now a big greasy kid who lived in a dorm room and wanted nothing to do with him.

Dog Day was about two brothers who volunteer at an animal shelter, and who organize an adoption parade with the dogs through downtown Scottsdale, Arizona. Drew struggled, his finger vainly pointed at each word.

"Reh . . . Reh . . . Ret . . ."

Wade was supposed to just let him sound the words out himself, but the wrinkles in the boy's forehead got to him. "Retriever," he finally said. "It's a kind of dog."

Drew closed the book and rested his hand on Wade's arm. "Can't I just bring the wolf book again next time?"

17

SONYA LEANED against the bar. All the chairs were up except Wade's. "So how much are we talking?"

Wade shrugged and acted as if he had to think about it. "Total worth?"

"Yeah. I'm just curious."

"Well, okay. Figure I'm going to lose almost half of it to the divorce, and I've still got restitution to deal with, and there's a civil suit we're about to settle . . ."

"How much?"

"I don't know. Exactly."

"Yes, you do."

Yes, he did. He took a drink of his whiskey. "Thirty," he said.

Sonya's eyes got huge. "*Million?*"

Of course, it was closer to forty. That's how much he figured to have left when the dust settled. He wondered why he
did that. Shaved off just a little bit. "Give or take," he said.

She covered her mouth.

"What's the matter?" Wade asked.

"I don't know," she said. "It's kind of . . . sick."

18

WADE REQUESTED a meeting with the second-grade
teacher, Mrs. Amundson. She was an attractive young
woman, maybe thirty, with curly black hair and a patient
smile. They sat after school on tiny plastic chairs in her classroom, surrounded by leaves pasted to construction paper.
Wade brought out the notebook he kept on the students'
progress.

"Marco is doing especially well. He seems to have a real
grasp of context and he's anticipating stories, which is pretty
high-level stuff. I'm not sure he even needs one-on-one attention. DeAndre—I don't know if he's been tested for dys-
lexia, but he really struggles with blocks of text and complex
sentences."

Mrs. Amundson nodded patiently.

Wade flipped to his report on Drew. "Finally, I'm not
sure what to make of Drew. He just keeps bringing the same
book, this wolf book; he's basically just memorized it. I want
him to be comfortable, but he's just repeating the story now.
I went online, and it looks like there are three more books in
that series. I thought if you could have the librarian request
the other books, I could work on some word-attack strategies
with him—"

The teacher looked up.

Wade shrugged. "I've been doing some research." He held out the notebook.

Mrs. Amundson took it. "This is very thorough, Mr.—"

"McAdam."

"Mr. McAdam." She looked down at his report. "Unfortunately, our district cut its library funding last year. We have no librarian. We're not allowed to request any new books."

He stared at her. "You can't request *books*? But this is a school."

"Yes." She smiled.

"So a kid gets hooked on a series and he's just . . . on his own? That's crazy."

She closed the notebook and looked up at him. "Look. This is very nice, what you've done. But I need to tell you, all of these boys already work with a reading specialist. I just sent them with you because they're boys who have no male relationships in their lives, and there are no male teachers at this school. I thought they should have some casual, normal time around a man. That's all."

She handed Wade back his little notebook.

19

"I CAN'T, Wade," Sonya said. "Just . . . please."

Wade's head felt like it was on a swivel. "I know," he said. "I'm sorry."

She turned away and started washing glasses.

Wade looked around the bar, at the chairs up on the tables. Then he looked down at the bill she'd left for him an hour ago. "I know," he said again. His eyes were bleary. He couldn't focus. The bill looked like it was for forty bucks. As

always, Sonya had only charged him for every other whiskey. He opened his wallet. He stared at the blossom of dull,
greenish-white bills. He took out three fifties, then a fourth,
and a fifth, and finally all of them. He set the money on the
bar and left.

20

WADE STOOD in the children's section of Auntie's Bookstore, staring at all the books. All the fucking books.

21

"I BROUGHT something for us," Wade said. He pulled
Drew up on his lap and took out the book he'd bought that
morning, the second in the series, *The Wolf and the River*. The
secretary cleared her throat, but Wade held the boy tight on
his lap, and this time he read the whole thing to Drew himself, working to keep his voice steady.

In the book, houses are going up in the fields around the
boy's family farm. Trees are being cut down, and the boy is
worried because the wolf has had a litter of six pups. At one
point, a bulldozer nearly takes out the wolf's den. Eventually
the boy buys a pool raft to help the wolf move her pups to the
safe side of the river, where there are no houses. On the last
five pages, as they cross the river, there are no words.

When Wade looked up, the secretary was walking across
the office toward them. She was bringing along the vice prin-
cipal, who was speaking angrily (" . . . the boy's on his *lap*!")
into her cell phone.

Wade hung on.

"And that's the end," Drew said.

WHEELBARROW KINGS

I'M HUNGRY AS FUCK.

Mitch knows a guy getting rid of a TV. A big-screen supposed to work great. Mitch says he watched UFC on it.

That don't make sense I say. A guy just giving away a big-screen.

Mitch says the guy has two TVs.

Mitch talks a lot of shit so I won't be surprised if there ain't no TV.

Fish and chips is what I really want. I got twelve dollars which would be plenty for fish and chips. So hungry.

Mitch says it's a heavy-ass TV and we'll need a wheelbarrow for sure.

I ask where the fuck are we supposed to get a wheelbarrow. Like I just carry a wheelbarrow around. Sometimes Mitch.

He says we'll pawn that TV for two hundred easy. Then I could spend my twelve bucks on fish and chips or steak or whatever the fuck I want.

Mitch's sister lives up on the south hill. He says she's got a wheelbarrow. She and her husband garden and shit. I met his sister one time. She seemed cool.

I started loving fish and chips when we had it at middle school. I never had it before that. I used to think chips were the different kind of fries with ridges like we had at school. But it can be any fries.

If we do get two hundred for that TV me and Mitch are gonna gear up over at Kittlestedt's. On Kittlestedt's icy shit. Get on a big old spark. None of that scungy east side peanut butter we been bulbing for a month now. Not after we sell that TV.

No more twelve-buck quarters for us.

We gonna amp up on a couple of fat bags Mitch says.

I'm hungry as fuck I say to Mitch.

We gonna eat for days after we sell that TV he says.

He wants to take a bus up the south hill to borrow his sister's wheelbarrow. Mitch has a bus pass. I got that twelve dollars but no way I want to spend a buck twenty-five on the bus. Because you can't even get east side shit for under twelve. Twelve is the cheapest I ever seen. Anywhere.

You comin Mitch asks.

If I do spend some of my money on the bus least I could eat then. Fish and chips. Or even just get a tacquito at Circle K and some Sun Chips. I like them Sun Chips too. But I ain't buying food unless we sell that TV.

Mitch's bus pass is expired. He wants me to pay for both of us on the bus. Fuck that I say. We get off. The bus drives away.

And I think of something. How the fuck are we gonna get that wheelbarrow all the way downtown from his sister's house anyway. It's like two miles. And we'd have to take the wheelbarrow back. Uphill.

Yeah that's true Mitch says.

I known that fucker two years. First time he ever said I was right.

First time you ever been right Mitch says.

Fuck I'm hungry.

You keep saying that. Fucking buy some food then Mitch says.

But he knows I can't. I need my twelve bucks. He's just fuckin jealous 'cause he ain't even got enough for a bump.

There's a coffee place downtown where I know this girl. I went to school with her. We walk down there. Keep our eyes open for wheelbarrows. You see wheelbarrows at construction sites sometimes it seems like. But when you need one you sure as fuck don't. I don't think there is a wheelbarrow in all of downtown Spokane.

The coffee shop has outside tables either side of the door. There's two guys in suits and sunglasses drinking ice coffee. They're eating scones. Them fucking scones look great. I'm hungry as shit. The business guys give me a look. Inside the coffee shop I lick my lips to get the salt.

The girl I know ain't working. Sometimes she gives me the day-old pastry. She'll say what happened to you Daryl. And I'll say what happened to you. I forget her name. She's kind of fat now. She wasn't fat in middle school. She was pretty hot I think. But she's fat now.

But that's not what I mean when I say what happened to you. About her being fat. I'm just fucking around. And I did know her name before. I just don't know it now.

Anyways it don't matter because she ain't working. Some guy is working instead. With a goatee. I ask him is the girl who works here around. He makes a face like what girl or maybe he just thinks Mitch and me stink. And he looks at the stain on my

T-shirt. I was having a hot dog at the Circle K a few days ago and I was with Todo and that fucker waits until you take a bite of something and then he says the funniest shit. He could be a stand-up comedian Todo. I forget what he said exactly but the ketchup squirted on my shirt. And then it left this stain.

Mitch flops down in a booth.

The goatee guy watches Mitch pick at his face. You have to order something if you're gonna stay here the coffee guy says. They got these cinnamon rolls must be half frosting. Fuck me I am so hungry. The goatee guy looks at me like I'm a fucking jerk-spazz.

That girl—I have to start over. And then her name comes. Marci! Marci said come in and she'd give me something from the day-olds. Marci. I can't stop blinking.

Marci's not here.

Can you check. Can you check if she left me something from the day-olds.

I am so fucking hungry.

A couple ladies with shopping bags come in.

The goatee dude rubs his head. He leans forward like he's telling me a secret. If I give you tweakers a scone will you get the fuck out of here.

Give us each one.

They got a day-old basket next to the register. The dude takes two scones and gives them to me. One is a triangle. That's the one I want.

Come on Mitch I say.

We go outside. It's funny. Them two business dudes are sitting there eating scones. And Mitch and me are eating scones. Only we didn't pay for ours. Who's the fucking smart guys now.

Only that scone ain't too good. It don't taste like nothing. Not like that cinnamon roll would've. Or like fish and chips. More like wood chips.

Fuck me. I'm even hungrier now.

Mitch and me decide to just walk to the dude with the TV's house. Maybe he's got a wheelbarrow Mitch says.

It's over the river in a big house I never seen before. A covered front porch with a fridge out front. There's like ten people hanging at the house but it ain't a party. Mitch says the dude is strictly into weed but there's a smoked lightbulb on the front porch. I think maybe we'll get hooked up here. But the dude with the TV is all business.

He's eating a Hot Pocket while he talks to us. Fuck me I want that Hot Pocket. So hungry.

You fucking stink this dude says to Mitch.

Yeah I'm gonna go home and get cleaned up after we sell that TV Mitch says.

What's wrong with this guy he asks.

He's just hungry Mitch says.

The dude's got a brand-new TV in the living room. Two little kids are on the PS2. They're playing *Call of Duty*. I'm good on that game I say but they don't look up. The TV is pretty big. How big is that TV I ask.

Fifty-five inch the dude says. He says that's his new TV. The Double Nickel he calls it. The Sammy Hagar.

The picture is too sharp though. It's like sharper than your eyes. That would freak me out. On *Call of Duty* I see shit I never knew was there. Life ain't that real.

The other TV is on the back porch. It ain't even plugged in. It's an old-school projector TV. I worried Mitch was full of shit. But here it is just like he said. This TV is the biggest TV

I ever seen. I don't even know how big. The thing's probably five feet tall and five feet wide. Probably three feet thick. It's huge. Like a room. Mitch is right we're gonna need a fucking wheelbarrow.

You want it it's yours says the dude who lives here.

You know anyone who has a wheelbarrow around here Mitch asks the dude.

He looks at Mitch like get your own fucking wheelbarrow.

There's an alley behind the dude's house so Mitch and me go walking along there looking for a wheelbarrow.

I am so fucking hungry. For a while in middle school we got free lunch. But then my mom worked at the air force base and we got off free lunch. She used to make me cold lunch. But whenever there was fish and chips I'd buy my own school lunch. That's how much I liked it. And chili. I liked the chili fine but I really liked them cinnamon rolls. It's funny they always had cinnamon rolls and chili in middle school. I don't know why. They just did.

Fuck. I am so hungry.

I'm gonna kick your ass you don't stop saying that Mitch says.

You can't kick my ass.

A ten-year-old girl could kick your fucking jittery ass.

That girl's six-year-old sister could kick your picker ass.

That girl's newborn baby sister could kick your smelly ass.

That girl's kitten could kick your ass.

That girl's kitten's fleas could kick your ass.

Sometimes Mitch cracks me up. He ain't no Todo but sometimes.

We walk down that alley. There's a kid's Big Wheel. There's a turned-over grocery cart but it's got busted wheels.

And that's when I see it. Hey Mitch look. No shit. Next to a fall-down garage in back of this house. Leaning up against it. It ain't even rusted. A goddamn almost brand-new wheelbarrow. You hear that saying My Lucky Day and I guess sometimes.

There's a little chain-link fence with bent poles. I climb it easy. Grab that wheelbarrow. I wheel it up and heft it over the fence to Mitch. We push that thing back down the alley. We're practically running.

We fucking feel like kings.

I get one-fifty and you get fifty Mitch says. Out of the blue like that.

That's bullshit. I went and got the wheelbarrow.

I knew where the TV was he says.

Don't be a dick Mitch. We both gotta push that thing to the pawn.

One-twenty and eighty.

Don't be a dick.

One-ten ninety.

Fine.

I'm so fucking starving. The TV dude is eating some pretzels out of a bag when we come back. He's standing in his backyard watching his matted dog scoot around on his itchy ass on the dirt. He's laughing like it was a TV show.

The TV dude looks up and sees us. He's surprised we found a wheelbarrow.

How come you don't grow grass back here Mitch asks. That would look better. I can hear in Mitch's voice he thinks we're the shit for getting a wheelbarrow so fast.

I don't suppose you got another one of them Hot Pockets I ask the TV dude.

Nah man. He offers me some pretzels and I take a handful. But they don't taste like nothing. Just the salt.

We leave the wheelbarrow at the bottom of the stairs by
the porch and go get on that TV. We can't barely budge it.
That fucking TV is the heaviest fucking thing I ever lifted. I
can't get under it and once we get it up we drop it.

Be fucking careful Mitch says.

You fucking be careful. You was pushing instead of lifting.

The TV dude just stands there eating his pretzels. Smiling
at us. Like he did with the dog with the itchy ass.

Mitch spits on his hands. You got anything else you want
to get rid of Mitch asks.

Get the fuck out of here. You guys smell like ass.

We pick it up again. We can't get a hold on it. It's all tippy.
But that two hundred bucks is out there so we muscle it down
the steps. It don't go in the wheelbarrow very well. Kind of
sits on top on the rim. And it weighs so much it flattens the
wheel. Fucking brand-new wheelbarrow and the wheel goes
almost totally flat.

Fuck Mitch says. You got a pump man?

Get the fuck out of here the TV dude says. Fuckin' chalkers.

So we push it down the alley and then down the street.
I'm on the front of the TV keeping it steady. Mitch is holding
the wood handles of the wheelbarrow and pushing. We go
really slow like that. A few feet for a minute and then we got
to stop. It would be easier if the wheel had more air. But it
still wouldn't be easy. I'm sweating. The sweat keeps getting
in my eyes.

Fuck Mitch says.

I know I say.

I'm balancing that TV and walking backward. One time

Mitch trips a little and the TV starts to go over and I just get in front of it. I keep it from going over. Motherfucker watch what you're doing I say.

Sorry Mitch says. I tripped. He gets on the TV too and we get it balanced again.

It's six blocks to the pawn. It probably takes us ten minutes to go a block. Some kids are riding bikes like sharks around us. They stop to watch. One of them is eating a sandwich.

Mitch has to stop to wipe his sweat and breathe. I'm crazy fucking hungry.

What kind of sandwich is that I ask the little kid. It looks like cheese but not with the cheese melted just slices of cheese on white bread.

Fuck off tweaker the kid says. And he rides away on his bike eating that cheese sandwich. Or whatever kind of sandwich it is.

I swear if I wasn't on this TV I would pull that kid off his fucking bike and beat his ass. We didn't talk to older guys that way when I was a kid.

The next block goes a little faster. I think of that girl at the coffee shop and I wonder if she gives me the day-olds so I'll leave like the goatee guy did. But I don't think so. I think she likes to talk to me.

She gave me a cinnamon roll one time. That's how I know they're so good there. Remember these in middle school I asked her but she didn't remember the cinnamon rolls. Anyways that cinnamon roll was sure better than them dry scones. I wonder why them businessmen would eat scones when they could afford cinnamon rolls or even oat bars or muffins. I wonder why the fuck they make scones in the first place.

Why the fuck you think they make scones at all I ask Mitch.

Great mystery Mitch says.

Sometimes he is as funny as Todo.

The third block goes even slower. Mitch's arms are shaking. Red splotchy covered with sweat. And I feel dizzy from all the walking backward. You gotta switch me Mitch says.

So I push for a few blocks and Mitch steadies. Only I don't trust his steadying so I push more carefully than he did. It yanks your arms out of their sockets pushing that wheelbarrow. And even though it's a pretty new wheelbarrow I get a sliver from the wood handles.

Fuck me I say. I got a sliver.

I got like a hundred.

You got a hundred slivers.

I said LIKE a hundred.

We get four blocks. Only two to go. We stop at this yard and take turns steadying while the other guy rests in the grass until this old guy comes out and yells get the fuck off my yard. I'm gonna call the cops.

Fucking call 'em then Mitch says.

Where'd you steal that TV the old guy says. He's waving something at us.

Fuck you Mitch says.

But for some reason I don't want the guy to think we stole it. We got it from a guy I say. And the wheelbarrow. Even though we didn't get that from a guy but stole it.

We start going again.

And I think of something. The old guy had a remote control. I say that to Mitch. You see that. I just thought of it. He was waving something at us and it was a fucking remote control.

Yeah Mitch says and we both laugh. Fucking people Mitch says.

Like a sword I say. He carries that remote around.

People spend their whole lives in front of that fucking box says Mitch. He says it like we got the life or something.

We're a few houses away from Monroe. The busy street with the pawn.

There's a Hawaiian grill place on Monroe just down from the pawn. They got this chicken and rice but it's at least five bucks. That sounds even better than fish and chips. That would leave me with just seven bucks though. Can't get no bump for seven bucks.

I think I'm gonna fucking starve to death Mitch. I'm dying here.

We're almost there he says.

Fucking kings.

By the time we get to the last block the whole tire has gone flat on the wheelbarrow. Now I'm just pushing on the steel rim. It's like pushing a fucking house uphill.

Pull motherfucker.

I am.

We can barely get it up on the sidewalk and then there's a curb cut and we can barely get up the other side of that. My hands are red raw. I been pushing the last three blocks. I should get half I say.

Fine Mitch says.

At the pawn I stay outside and steady the TV while Mitch goes inside. Some dude is coming out as Mitch goes in. He just bought a circular saw. He laughs at me. That's the funniest thing I ever saw he says. Fucking tweaker standing with a giant old TV on a wheelbarrow. And he takes out his phone and takes a picture of me.

I don't care. I just smile for the picture. 'Cause we made

it. Fuck the TV dude and the little kid with the sandwich and that old guy with the remote and this guy with the camera phone. My big problem now is whether to have fish and chips or that Hawaiian chicken and rice.

The pawn guy comes out with a big-ass grin on his face. He stares at that TV like he can't believe we pushed it all the way there. It is pretty fucking cool now that I think about it. All the shit we went through. Fucking day this was.

How far did you guys push this thing?

A mile Mitch says.

This kind of pisses me off. It's enough what we done without making up some story. Six blocks I say.

No shit. And he shakes his head like we come from the North Pole or something.

It works great Mitch says. I just watched UFC on it this morning.

That pawn dude has the biggest grin on. Follow me he says.

I don't want to leave it here I say. It might fall.

The pawn dude helps us lean it against the wall of the store.

Then he takes us inside to where there's ten TVs hanging up. Most of them are flat and big like that TV dude's new double nickel. They're all plugged in. They all work good. Them new TVs are like two hundred bucks is all.

You guys see any big-console projection-screen TVs in here.

We say we don't.

No transistor radios or VHS players either. You guys are like five years late. I couldn't GIVE that fucking dinosaur away. I couldn't give it away if it came with a free car and a blowjob. Now get the fuck out of my store.

In front of the pawn Mitch and I got nothing to say. We just stare at each other. Mitch looks sorry. He probably thinks I blame him. But I don't. Fuck he didn't know. It was a good try. A lot of things are like that. Good tries. I just wish I wasn't so fucking hungry. And I wish I had enough for Mitch's bump too and for some fish and chips. But I don't. I just got the twelve bucks. Mitch knows. He looks like he's gonna die. Pale as shit.

Tell you what. We look back. The pawn dude is standing there. He's been watching us. I'll give you ten bucks for the wheelbarrow.

Fifteen Mitch says.

It's got a flat fucking tire the guy says. But he smiles. Like he's watching that dog rub its ass. Okay he says. Fifteen.

You gotta take the TV too I say.

What am I the fucking United Way the pawn guy says. Fine. Take it round back and put it in the alley. So we lift it again off the wheelbarrow. It's like needles in my back every step we take with that fucking TV. My face is pressed against the black console which is a thousand degrees from the sun. My hands are so sweaty I'm sure I'm gonna drop it. But we make it to the alley where we leave it with a bunch of other garbage. Wire. Old shopping carts. An axle.

The guy gives Mitch fifteen bucks. You guys know I'm doing you a favor he says. I'm not gonna get fifteen bucks for that wheelbarrow. You know that right.

Yeah we say.

Good he says. Then since I'm doing you a favor you can do me one. Next time you cat shit–smelling motherfuckers get some idea to steal something and pawn it you go to a different fucking store. Right? Go to Double Eagle over on Division. Fuckin' chalkers the pawn dude says.

Mitch goes to give me half of the fifteen but I say that's okay. We each got twelve bucks now. Plus three left over. We ain't making it to Kittlestedt's but that's okay. We'll go over to the east side where a fucker can still be king for twelve.

And that leaves us three bucks to eat on. It ain't enough for no fucking fish and chips. But we got enough for the Circle K.

Kings.

Mitch gets a pepperoni stick. I get a ninety-nine-cent big bag of Sun Chips. And we split a Dr. Pepper. The clerk wrinkles his nose but fuck him.

Then Mitch and me start walking toward the east side. I wish I would have thought to ask that coffee shop guy when that girl works again. The one who I went to middle school with. Fuck me. I think I forgot her name again.

I can't even taste the fucking Sun Chips. It's like they got no taste at all.

Then Mitch starts telling the whole story. Remember that free scone you got us.

Like I wasn't even there. Yeah I say.

And you saw that fucking wheelbarrow like you blew out your birthday candles and wished for it.

I laugh at that. Yeah.

And we come back and that fucking dog is scooting on his ass. And even though I was there for all of it I laugh at every fucking thing he tells me about our day. We walk and Mitch tells the whole fucking story again. I think he's gonna tell that story forever. And I didn't laugh once when we were doing that shit. But now it all seems so fucking funny I can't hardly stand it.

I guess remembering is better than living.

And what about that dude waving his remote control Mitch says.

Yeah what the fuck was that.

Maybe he was a fucking Jedi knight Mitch says and we gotta stop walking we're laughing so hard. Fucking Ben Kenobi I say. And we both bend over laughing. And fuck me it's nice to be out walking. To have twelve bucks in your pocket and some tasteless Sun Chips in your belly. We walk and we laugh. All the way over to the east side.

STATISTICAL ABSTRACT
FOR MY HOMETOWN OF
SPOKANE, WASHINGTON

1. The population of Spokane, Washington, is
    203,268. It is the 104th biggest city in the United
    States.

2. Even before the great recession, in 2008, 36,000
    people in Spokane lived below the poverty
    line—a little more than 18 percent of the popula-
    tion. That's about the same percentage as Wash-
    ington, D.C. at the time. The poverty rate was
    12.5 percent in Seattle.

3. Spokane is sometimes called the biggest city
    between Seattle and Minneapolis, but this is only
    true if you ignore everything below Wyoming,
    including Salt Lake City, Denver, Phoenix, and at
    least four cities in Texas.

4. This is really just another way of saying nobody
    much lives in Montana or the Dakotas.

5. My grandfather arrived in Spokane in the 1930s,
    on a freight train he'd jumped near Fargo. Even
    he didn't want to live in the Dakotas.

6. On any given day in Spokane, Washington, there
    are more adult men per capita riding children's
    BMX bikes than in any other city in the world.

7. I've never been sure where these guys are going
    on these little bikes, their knees up around their
    ears as they pedal. They all wear hats—ball caps
    in summer, stocking caps in winter. I've never
    been sure, either, whether the bikes belong to
    their kids or if they've stolen them. It may be that
    they just prefer BMX bikes to ten-speeds. Many
    of them have lost their driver's licenses after too
    many DUIs.

8. I was born in Spokane in 1965. Beginning in
    about 1978, when I was thirteen, I wanted to
    leave.

9. I'm still here.

10. In 2000 and 2001, the years I most desperately
    wanted to move out of Spokane, 2,632 illegal

aliens were deported by the Spokane office of the U.S. Border Patrol. They were throwing people out of Spokane and I *still* couldn't leave.

11. In 1978, I had a BMX bike. It didn't have a chain guard, and since I favored bellbottom jeans, my pant legs were constantly getting snagged. This would cause me to pitch over the handlebars and into the street. My cousin stole that bike once, but he pretended he'd just borrowed it without my permission and eventually he gave it back. Later on it was stolen for good by an older guy in my neighborhood named Steve. I was in my front yard afterward, being lectured by my father for leaving my bike out unprotected, when I saw Steve go tooling past our house on the bike he'd just stolen from me. Stocking cap on his head, knees up around his ears. I was too scared to say anything. Fear has often overtaken me during such situations. I hated myself for that. Far more than I hated Steve.

12. In 1978, Spokane's biggest employer was Kaiser Aluminum. My dad worked there. Kaiser went belly-up in the 1990s, after it was bought by a corporate raider. All of the retirees, my dad included, lost a chunk of their pensions. Now all of the biggest employers in Spokane are government entities. Technically, *I* haven't held a job

since 1994. This does not make me unique in my
hometown.

13.   One of the poorest elementary schools in the
       state of Washington is in Spokane. In fact, it's
       right behind my house. At one time, 98 percent
       of its students got free and reduced-price lunch. I
       sometimes think about the 2 percent who didn't
       get free lunch. When I was a kid, we lived for two
       years on a ranch near Springdale, on the border of
       the Spokane Indian Reservation. My dad com-
       muted sixty miles each way to the aluminum plant.
       On the third day of school, in 1974, a kid leaned
       over to me on the bus and said, "What's the deal,
       Richie, you gonna wear different clothes to school
       every day?" Because of my dad's job, my siblings and
       I were the only kids in school who didn't get free
       lunch *and* free breakfast. At home, we had Cream
       of Wheat. At school they had Sugar Pops.

14.   Sugar Pops tasted way better than Cream of
       Wheat. In 1974, my dad got laid off from the
       aluminum plant and we *still* didn't qualify for free
       breakfast. You must have had to be really poor to
       get Sugar Pops.

15.   Now they're called Corn Pops. Who in their
       right mind would rather eat Corn Pops than
       Sugar Pops?

16. While it's true that I don't technically have a job and that I live in a poor neighborhood, I don't mean to make myself sound poor. I do pretty well.

17. In Spokane it doesn't matter where you live, or how big your house is—you're never more than three blocks from a bad neighborhood. I've grown to like this. In a lot of cities, especially in Spokane's more affluent neighbors, Seattle and Portland, it can be easier to insulate yourself from poverty; you can live miles away from any poor people and start to believe that everyone is as well-off as you are.

18. They are not.

19. The median family income in Spokane, Washington, is $51,000 a year. In Seattle, the median family income is $88,000 a year. Point: Seattle.

20. In Seattle, though, the median house price is $308,000. In Spokane it is $181,000.

21. Drivers in Spokane spend a total of 1.8 million hours a year stuck in traffic on the freeway. This is an average of five hours a year per person in the metropolitan region. In Seattle, they spend 72 million hours stuck on the freeway, an average of

twenty-five hours per person in the region. That's an entire day. Suck on that, Seattle.

22. What would it take for you to willingly surrender an entire day of your life?

23. This used to be my list of reasons why I didn't like Spokane: a) It is too poor, too white, and too un-educated. b) There is not enough ethnic food. c) It has a boring downtown and no art-house theater and is too conservative.

24. In the past few years, though, the downtown has been revitalized, the art scene is thriving, and the food has gotten increasingly better. There are twenty Thai and Vietnamese restaurants listed in the Yellow Pages. The art-house theater reopened at a time when similar theaters were closing everywhere else. There are bike paths everywhere, and I keep meeting cool, progressive people. The city even went for Obama in '08—barely, but still. The weather is wonderful, outdoor opportunities abound, and the people are incredibly friendly.

25. For the most part, despite all that, Spokane is still poor, white, and uneducated.

26. My own neighborhood is among the poorest in the state. It has an inordinate number of halfway

houses, shelters, group homes, and drug- and alcohol-rehab centers.

27. I remember back when I was a newspaper reporter, I covered a hearing filled with South Hill homeowners, men and women from old-money Spokane, vociferously complaining about a group home going into their neighborhood. They were worried about falling property values, rising crime, and "undesirables." An activist I spoke to called these people NIMBYs. It was the first time I'd heard the term. I thought he meant NAMBLA—the North American Man/Boy Love Association. That seemed a little harsh to me.

28. Bedraggled and beaten women, women carrying babies and followed by children, sometimes walk past my house on their way to the shelters and group homes. Often they carry their belongings in ragged old suitcases. Sometimes in garbage sacks.

29. Poverty and crime are linked, of course. Spokane's crime rate is well above the national average, and ranks the city 114th among the four hundred largest American cities, just below Boston. There are about ten murders a year, and 1,100 violent crimes. There are almost 12,000

property crimes—theft and burglary, that sort of thing. One year, a police sergeant estimated that a thousand bikes had been reported stolen.

30. I believe it.

31. My wife looked out the window at two in the morning once and saw a guy riding a child's BMX bike while dragging another one behind him. He was having trouble doing this, and eventually he laid one bike down in the weeds. I called the police and crouched by the window all night, watching until they arrested him when he came back for the second bike. I felt great, like McGruff the Crime Dog.

32. Another time, before I was married, I had gone for a bike ride and was sitting on my stoop with my bike propped against the railing when a guy tried to steal it. He just climbed on and started riding away. With me sitting there. I chased him down the block and grabbed the frame and he hopped off. "Sorry," he said, "I thought it was mine." What could I say? "Well . . . it isn't."

33. Another time, we hired a tree trimmer who showed up with three day laborers in the back of his pickup truck. One of them disappeared after only an hour of work. The tree trimmer didn't

seem concerned; he said workers often wandered off if the work was too hard. It wasn't until the next day that I realized the day laborer had made his escape on my unlocked mountain bike. I'd paid only $25 for that one, at a pawn shop where I was looking, in vain, for my previous bike, which had also been stolen. Since pawn-shop bikes have almost always been stolen from somewhere, it seemed somehow fitting that it would be stolen again.

34. A friend's rare and expensive bike once went missing and showed up for sale on Craigslist. I drove with him to meet the seller. We made this elaborate plan that involved the two of us stealing the bike back, or confronting the thieves, or something like that. I just remember I was supposed to wait in the car until he gave me a signal. When we arrived at their house we discovered that the bike thieves were huge, all tatted up, and shirtless. They were sitting on a couch on their porch, drinking malt liquor, and smoking. I waited for the signal. A few minutes later my friend got back in the car. It wasn't his bike. He was disappointed. I was tremendously relieved.

35. The largest number of people I ever saw walking to one of the shelters in my neighborhood was five: a crying woman and her four children, all

behind her, like ducklings. I smiled encouragingly
at them. It was a hot day. I had the sprinkler on
in my front yard and the last duckling stepped
into the oscillating water and smiled at me. I
don't know why the whole thing made me feel so
crappy, but it did.

36. Once, when I was watching sports on TV, a guy
    pounded on our front door and started yelling,
    "Tiffany! Goddamn it, Tiffany! Get your ass
    down here!"

37. I went to the door. The guy was wearing torn
    jeans and no shirt and a ball cap. He seemed
    sketchy and twitchy, like a meth user. I said there
    was no one inside named Tiffany. He said, "I
    know this is a shelter for women and I know she's
    here." I insisted that it wasn't a shelter, that the
    place he was looking for was miles away, and that
    I was going to call the police if he didn't leave.

38. He said he was going to kick my ass. I tried to
    look tough, but I was terrified.

39. My lifetime record in fistfights is zero wins, four
    losses, and one draw. I used to claim the draw as
    a win, but my brother, who witnessed that fight,
    always made this face like, *Really?*

40. The shirtless guy looking for Tiffany swore col-
     orfully at me. Then he climbed on a little kid's
     BMX bike and rode away, his knees hunched up
     around his ears.

41.   Later, when I was sure he was gone, I went to the
     shelter and knocked on the front door. A woman's
     voice came from a nearby window. "Yes?" she
     said. I couldn't see her face. I told her what had
     happened. She thanked me. I left.

42. For days, I imagined the other things I could have
     said to that asshole. Or I imagined punching him.
     I felt like I'd not handled it well, although I don't
     know what I should have done differently.

43. After that, I decided to volunteer at the shelter. I'd
     always seen kids playing behind the high fence,
     and I thought I could play with them or read
     to them. But I was told they only had a small
     number of male volunteers because having men
     around made so many of the women nervous.

44. Of the 36,000 people living in poverty in Spo-
     kane, most are children.

45. Right at the peak of my obnoxious and conde-
     scending loathing for my hometown, I rented a
     houseboat in Seattle for $900 a month so I could

pretend I lived there. While staying on that boat,
and hanging around Seattle, I had a conversation
with someone about all that was wrong with Spokane. He said that it was too poor and too white
and too uneducated and too unsophisticated, and
as he spoke, I realized something: this guy hated
Spokane because of people like me. *I* grew up
poor, white, and unsophisticated, the first in my
family to graduate from college. And worse, I had
made the same complaints. Did I hate Spokane
. . . or did I hate *myself*? Was this just a kind of
self-loathing? Then I had this even more sobering
thought: Was I the kind of snob who hates a place
because it's poor?

46. I think there are only two things you can do with
     your hometown: look for ways to make it better,
     or look for another place to live.

47. Last year I volunteered at the low-income school
     behind my house, tutoring kids who needed
     help with reading. Most of the other tutors were
     retired, and it was sweet to watch the six-year-
     olds take these smiling seniors by the hands and
     drag them around the school, looking for a quiet
     place to read. One day I was helping this intense
     little eight-year-old, Dylan. We read a story
     together about a cave boy who was frightened by
     a wolf until the wolf saves his life and becomes

his friend. Every time I showed up after that, Dylan had the wolf book out for me to read. I'd say, "You should get another book," and he'd say, "Why should I read another book when this one's so good?" Point: Dylan.

48. One day we talked about what scared us. After I told Dylan how I used to be afraid of the furnace in our basement, Dylan told me he was scared that his brother would kill him. I laughed at the commonalities of all people and told him that brothers just sometimes fight with each other, it wasn't anything to be afraid of, his brother loved him, and he said, "No, my brother really tried to kill me. He choked me and I passed out and my stepfather had to tear him off me. I was in the hospital. He still says he's gonna kill me one day." I reported this to the teacher, who said the boy's brother had indeed tried to kill him.

49. The Halloween before last, I glanced out the window and saw a woman making her way past the front of my house with a toddler in her arms. I grabbed the candy bowl, thinking they were trick-or-treating, and that's when I noticed a young man walking beside the woman. I noticed him because out of nowhere, he punched her. She swerved sideways but kept limping down the street. I dropped the candy and ran outside.

"Hey!" I yelled. "Leave her alone!" Now I could
see the woman was crying, carrying crutches in
one hand and a three-year-old boy in the other.
Her boyfriend, or whoever he was, was red with
anger. He ignored me and kept yelling at her.
"Your mom told me you were coming here! Now
stop! I just wanna talk to you! You can't do this!"
I stepped between them. "Leave her alone!" I said
again; then I said, "Get outta here!" He balled his
hands into fists and said, "That ain't happenin'."
But during all of this he refused to look at me,
as if I weren't even there. His eyes were red and
bleary. I was terrified. I told him he just needed
to go home. He wouldn't acknowledge me. He
kept stepping to the side to get an angle on his
girlfriend, and I kept stepping in front of him. At
some point the woman handed me her crutches
so she could get a better hold of her child. She
was limping heavily. We air-danced down the
block this way, painfully slowly, silently: her, me,
him. Eventually I said, "Look, I'm gonna call
the cops and this is all gonna get worse." His
face went white. Then he tensed up and took a
short, compact swing. At himself. It sounded like
a gunshot, the sound of his fist hitting his own
face. It was loud enough that my neighbor, Mike,
came outside. Mike is a big, strapping Vietnam
veteran, about as tough and as reasonable a man
as I know. The guy seemed worried by Mike, cer-

tainly more worried than he'd been by me. Mike
and I stood on either side of the woman until her
angry young boyfriend gave up and stalked off.
Twice more he punched himself as he walked. He
was sobbing. We waited until he was gone and
then we escorted her to the shelter. All the way
there, the little boy stared at me. I didn't know
what to say. For some reason I asked if he was going trick-or-treating later that night. His mother
looked at me like I was crazy.

50. At the shelter, I gave her back the crutches. The
woman knocked on the door. It opened. Mike and
I stayed on the street, because that's as close as
we're supposed to get. Maybe as close as we want
to get. A gentle hand took the woman's arm and
she and her boy were led carefully inside.

ACKNOWLEDGMENTS

These stories, published over the last seven years, had the good fortune of falling under the pens of some terrific editors. I want to single out two who are also friends, and who generously treat writers with the same exacting care they bring to their own work. Sam Ligon published a few of my stories at *Willow Springs*, read most of the others, and shared with me his laser-like ability to hone lines and find stories. Amy Grace Loyd displayed the same remarkable touch with prose that she does with people, and like other writers she's edited at *Playboy* and *Byliner*, I'm better for having experienced both.

My deep thanks to two other good friends, my editor Cal Morgan, tireless champion of story writers, distracted novelists, and other misfits, and my agent Warren Frazier, the literary social worker who found homes for these troubled kids. Thanks also to a slew of fine editors and writers: Jordan Bass at *McSweeney's*, Christopher Beha at *Harper's*, Mary Morgan at *Fugue*, Kevin Sampsell, Joseph Mattson, Peter Wild, Tom Perrotta, Heidi Pitlor of *The Best American Short Stories*, and Dave Eggers and the crew of *The Best American Nonrequired Reading*. Thanks also to Anne Walter, Shawn Vestal, Dan Butterworth, and the staff of the Richard Hugo House in Seattle for the assignment that became "Don't Eat Cat."

JESS WALTER

BEAUTIFUL RUINS

The No. 1 *New York Times* Bestseller

The story begins in 1962. Somewhere on a rocky patch of the sun-drenched Italian coastline a young innkeeper, chest-deep in daydreams, looks out over the incandescent waters of the Ligurian Sea and views an apparition: a beautiful woman, a vision in white, approaching him on a boat. She is an American starlet, he soon learns, and she is dying.

And the story begins again today, half a world away in Hollywood, when an elderly Italian man shows up on a movie studio's back lot searching for the woman he last saw at his hotel fifty years before.

Gloriously inventive, funny, tender and constantly surprising, *Beautiful Ruins* is a novel full of fabulous and yet very flawed people, all of them striving towards another sort of life, a future that is both delightful and yet, tantalizingly, seems just out of reach.

'Magic...A monument to crazy love with a deeply romantic heart' *New York Times*

'A novel shot in sparkly Technicolor' *Booklist*

'Hilarious and compelling' *Esquire*

JESS WALTER

THE FINANCIAL LIVES OF THE POETS

Meet Matt Prior. He's about to lose his job, his house, his wife, and maybe his sanity too.

Financial journalist Matt quit his job to set up a website which couldn't fail. Only now he's woken up to the biggest crisis since the Great Crash, and it has. He's got six days to save his house. It's hard to focus when your wife's having an online affair with her childhood sweetheart, but there are children to think about . . . So when he gets hold of some high-grade dope and finds he can sell a piece on at a profit, he begins to think this might be his salvation.

A fabulously funny, heartfelt novel about how we can skate close to the edge of ruin - and pull back.

'A beautifully laid-back exultation of the human connections that make life worth living' *Metro*

'Ecstatically funny and unusually big-hearted' *Financial Times*

'It made me laugh more than any other book I've read this year' Nick Hornby

He just wanted a decent book to read ...

Not too much to ask, is it? It was in 1935 when Allen Lane, Managing Director of Bodley Head Publishers, stood on a platform at Exeter railway station looking for something good to read on his journey back to London. His choice was limited to popular magazines and poor-quality paperbacks – the same choice faced every day by the vast majority of readers, few of whom could afford hardbacks. Lane's disappointment and subsequent anger at the range of books generally available led him to found a company – and change the world.

'We believed in the existence in this country of a vast reading public for intelligent books at a low price, and staked everything on it'
Sir Allen Lane, 1902–1970, founder of Penguin Books

The quality paperback had arrived – and not just in bookshops. Lane was adamant that his Penguins should appear in chain stores and tobacconists, and should cost no more than a packet of cigarettes.

Reading habits (and cigarette prices) have changed since 1935, but Penguin still believes in publishing the best books for everybody to enjoy. We still believe that good design costs no more than bad design, and we still believe that quality books published passionately and responsibly make the world a better place.

So wherever you see the little bird – whether it's on a piece of prize-winning literary fiction or a celebrity autobiography, political tour de force or historical masterpiece, a serial-killer thriller, reference book, world classic or a piece of pure escapism – you can bet that it represents the very best that the genre has to offer.

Whatever you like to read – trust Penguin.

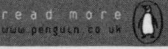